Praise for *Imagine Your Life Like This*

"The stories in *Imagine Your Life Like This* are unforgettable, with characters deftly portrayed, sometimes with a single memorable line. They have outsize vices, married men, and cookie binging. They lie, they steal, they act on violent impulses, yet I loved them and longed for redemption for each and every one. You want to believe that light boxes might solve their north-country-long-winter problems, but they know deep down that's not true. I particularly connected with the sardonic, vulnerable women. They hide from the truth for a while, but inevitably truth is as necessary to them as a good meal, a strong drink. Brava, Sarah Layden!"—Patricia Henley, author of *Other Heartbreaks* and *Hummingbird House*

"A great collection of short stories can make you feel as though the writer is taking you on a tour of a specific place and time, like a novel, while focusing on the many individual lives that make up the whole. *Imagine Your Life Like This* is one of those books: a wise and deeply satisfying collection that illuminates the courage and humor of ordinary people in a place where a mountain of broken glass in the moonlight can be more beautiful than Christmas lights, and a yearbook photo can illuminate the kindness that saved your life. I loved these stories. I was sorry when one ended but always, and immediately, drawn in by the next."—Susan Neville, author of *The Town of Whispering Dolls*

"Layden's vividly drawn characters struggle to define themselves in relation to who they used to be, who they want to be, and who others imagine them to be. In the midst of their various crises, they behave badly, make mistakes, and want what they can't have, and yet in spite of—or maybe because of—their fallibility, they remain sympathetic and lovable. *Imagine Your Life Like This* is a crisp, compassionate, and moving examination of the difficulty of seeing ourselves clearly and the pain of being seen by others in ways we can't control."—Ashley Wurzbacher, author of *Happy Like This*

Imagine Your Life Like This

SARAH LAYDEN

THE UNIVERSITY OF WISCONSIN PRESS

The University of Wisconsin Press
728 State Street, Suite 443
Madison, Wisconsin 53706
uwpress.wisc.edu

Gray's Inn House, 127 Clerkenwell Road
London EC1R 5DB, United Kingdom
eurospanbookstore.com

Printed in the United States of America
This book may be available in a digital edition.

Library of Congress Cataloging-in-Publication Data

Names: Layden, Sarah, author.
Title: Imagine your life like this / Sarah Layden.
Description: Madison, Wisconsin : The University of Wisconsin Press, 2023.
Identifiers: LCCN 2022028895 | ISBN 9780299342548 (paperback)
Subjects: LCGFT: Fiction. | Short stories.
Classification: LCC PS3612.A95845 I43 2023 | DDC 813/.6—dc23/eng/20220819
LC record available at https://lccn.loc.gov/2022028895

This is a work of fiction. Names, characters, places, and incidents either
are the product of the author's imagination or are used fictitiously,
and any resemblance to actual persons living or dead, businesses,
companies, events, or locales is entirely coincidental.

The following stories were previously published in slightly different form:
"Hysterectomy," *Stone Canoe*; "Resuscitation" and "Nothing and Nobody,"
Blackbird; "I'm Not Who You Think I Am" and "White Hands," *Zone 3*;
"Locations without Maps," *Evansville Review*; "Miller Miller,"
Artful Dodge; and "In Search Of," *42opus*.

For my mother

Contents

Imagine Your
Life Like This

Imagine Your Life Like This

If the Crab Shack were a ship, Annie would be the mermaid figurehead at the prow. Hair blown back by the double doors opening off Route 52, legs confined by a short pencil skirt. High heels even though her calves and ankles ached. Breasts, yes. Unlike the elaborately carved mermaids of yore, hers were covered by low-cut silk blouses. In truth, a polyblend.

The idea, Phil said, was to make people feel fancy about going out to eat. That was Annie's job, her presence fancifying decades-old tile, pocked and chair-leg scraped, and lending class to the signboard featuring a car-toonish trawler chuffing along. At the Crab Shack, nowhere near an ocean in any direction, the lights were dimmed out of necessity. Cheap bulbs that made Annie look sallow, which she resented each time she walked past the netting-draped mirror to grab laminated menus with full-color photos. Some diners would order by pointing at the pictures, unwilling to engage further. Like they were quiet and powerful fishermen, even if the seafood arrived frozen off a truck from Chicago. Phil, sitting on her couch after closing, was like, Jeez, Annie, give them a break. They're tired from working all week. They can act how they want. Phil tried to give her a back rub, and she sidled away. She thought but did not say: I can act how I want, too.

She was back in school, for one thing, after flunking out fifteen years ago. She would manage her shifts and classes better this time around. She had a duffel bag with her clothes and makeup case in the car. Now, on her way to class, she wore jeans and sneakers and imagined her younger class-mates seeing her in spike heels and miniskirt instead. They would proba-bly think she was a secretary and ask her to waive the bursar hold on their registration. Then they would realize, Oh, Annie—it's you! (Never mind that they didn't know her name yet.) Do you work here? And she would say No, I'm the head hostess of a restaurant. But she wouldn't say which one. Phil had given her free appetizer cards to pass out to students. They were rubber-banded in her backpack.

The first time around, she had failed all the courses she now found fascinating: Sociology, Intro to Art History, Spanish, Biology 1. Now she would take notes through every lecture and recitation, her hand a pale fluttering flag throughout the class period. She tried to forget about before, back when she couldn't have been bothered. In those days, Jackson was the only thing on her mind. When she would see him, and where they would get an apartment for which she'd buy new bath mats and doormats, and sure, it was a long commute to school, even further from her family, and then she was missing classes, and Jackson said, Hey, what's the point, anyway? She couldn't find an answer. He was seven years older. Handsome in a menacing way.

Enough. She didn't want to think about her ex-husband. Her first anthropology class of the semester was in ten minutes, and she sailed across the quad, skirting two large buildings that housed lecture auditoriums, and up three flights of stairs. Her bag was still light—she was waiting on payday to buy textbooks. If this large public university were a ship, she would be the one swabbing the decks. Last class of the day, then back to the Crab Shack. Where she did not swab anything, not in her nice clothes and heels.

On the door of the anthropology classroom was a handwritten note: *Prof. Lang is ill and will not be in class this afternoon.* A hand reached over Annie's shoulder and grabbed the piece of paper. Annie jumped as a woman's wrist grazed her hair.

"We must jettison this posthaste," the woman said, crumpling the note.

"Professor Lang?" Annie asked, recovering her composure to gaze skyward at her new instructor, who was nearly six feet tall and swathed in scarves and a flowy skirt. She jangled when she walked, large silver hoop earrings swaying as she tossed the paper into the classroom trash bin. Annie stared. Why not just say *throw away*?

"Me?" she said. "Heavens, no, and thank God for that. Professor Lang has gone mental. Which I suppose is a form of 'ill.' But the good professor won't be in class again, let alone this afternoon. At least not in this institution. Oops. Bad choice of words." Annie wondered if that was a joke. After a handful of students sauntered in, headphones screwed deeply into ear canals, the professor clapped her hands together briskly and commanded, "Let's begin."

There was an audible sigh. It was a beautiful fall-crisp day, a new beginning, and these teenagers already were beaten down by routine. Annie was unsympathetic. If her job at the Crab Shack had taught her anything, it was that sometimes life was trash, but you had to stand up straight and smile anyway. Even if the customers didn't notice or care. Even if the place smelled like a stagnant beach. Even if your manager loved you one day and hated you the next; Annie counseled a whole fleet of waitresses out by the dumpster in the parking lot. They would smoke cigarettes and talk about what else they'd rather be doing. Now Annie was dating the manager, Phil, whom she overheard Maya call a walking flip side of a "would you rather" drinking game. Would you rather drink from the grease trap or go out with Phil? Maya was bitter—Phil didn't put up with insubordination or slacking, and she was on notice for both. Do your job and your manager was a nonissue. And he was fine as a boyfriend, Annie had said to herself then, and many times since. He had talked about moving in together, and she demurred, offering school as an excuse. We'll probably see each other a little less, she told him, especially at exam time. School comes first, he had said, saluting her.

The professor messily sheafed through an armful of more syllabi than attendance warranted. "It seems the good Professor Lang had many plans for us," she said. "I was just called in, so you'll understand if I haven't exactly sorted this out."

In the doorway, a man with long dreadlocks appeared. He wore a replica Woodstock T-shirt, cargos, and combat boots. "Need a teaching assistant?" he asked.

The professor's face glowed. "Oh! Cliff. Good to see you. You'd be a wonderful TA. Alas, I have no budget or authority."

He gave a good-natured shrug and left. Professor Gregory turned back to the students as if surprised to see them there. A lanky boy who had folded himself into a desk raised his hand. "So. Who *are* you?"

She paused to consider. "Why, I'm nobody. Who are you?"

He lowered his hand. "Um, Kyle?" he said.

"You don't sound very sure," she said. "Interesting. I am Lucinda Gregory. You may call me Lucinda, or Ms. Gregory."

"How about Professor Gregory?" asked a girl with a perfectly straight blowout and tiny nose ring.

"Lucinda, or Ms. Gregory," repeated Lucinda Gregory.

"You mean you're not a professor?"

Lucinda carried the stack of semi-sorted pages to the far side of the room, as if to begin distribution. She had inherited a small class, less than a dozen students. With a *ta-da* flourish, she dumped the syllabi and Dr. Lang's lesson plans into the trash can. Her poor aim sent several pages over the side and onto an empty desk. She didn't notice.

"What does it mean," she mused, "to mean something?"

"Oh boy," muttered Nose Ring Girl.

"Case in point," Lucinda Gregory said. "Why 'Oh boy' and not 'Oh girl'? You are, after all, a girl. A woman. What's your name?"

"Chelsea," she said, like an accusation.

"So, Chelsea: What makes you use an expression that has little to nothing to do with you?"

The girl nervously touched her nose ring, then picked up her pen. She wrote nothing down. "It's just something people *say*," she said.

"Yes, but why? Why, why, why? That, students, is what I want you to explore in this class. The whys and the wherefores. The reasons behind the things you say and do. And then write it down. Fieldwork. Exploration. Ethnography!"

Kyle stared incredulously around the room and caught Annie's eye. She shrugged. Just because she was the oldest student in the room didn't mean she had to be translator. Anyway, she was similarly bewildered.

"I thought this was Intro to Anthro," Kyle said.

Lucinda sighed with theatrical flair. She stalked over to the trash can and picked out a single syllabus. Examining it, she tore the header off the first page, then tore it again to remove Dr. Lang's name and contact information. She waved the slip of paper, INTRODUCTION TO ANTHROPOLOGY, ANT IOI, like a tattered little flag.

"I can see you need proof," she said. "Anybody else? I've got more."

Annie gave a nervous laugh. She was in no way qualified to teach anything, yet imagined that she had more authority than her professor, who refused to commit to the title. Rank mattered. When somebody asked to see the manager at the Crab Shack, Annie got Phil. Let him deal with the disgruntled masses. Annie had worked there so long that she had everyone's cell numbers, a key to the supply closet and another to Phil's office, and was the emergency captain for fire drills. Maybe she wasn't running the ship, but damned if she wasn't facing forward at the helm, the good luck charm closest to the danger, who saw everything coming and went through it first. She couldn't have moved if she wanted to. Who else would welcome the customers?

Slow night at the Crab Shack, with at least three tables of single diners who rebuffed any conversation. Annie grabbed her new green notebook from beneath the reservation blotter and tried to come up with interview questions for herself as per Lucinda's worrisomely vague instructions. Start with the essentials, Lucinda had said. Ask yourself the most essential question you can think of.

The essentials in Annie's life: She had been terrified of going back to college. Years ago, Jackson had laughed when she confessed that she longed to do something other than work at a restaurant. Maybe be a nurse or a dental hygienist. Something with a future, you know? "You want to look inside people's mouths? You want to wipe their butts? Forget that. It's disgusting. You'd come home smelling like other people's bodies." Jackson worked construction and came home smelling like other people's houses. The two of them lived in a two-bedroom apartment off the interstate. The complex was nice enough. It had a pool. A covered parking space for Jackson's pickup. In the years since they split, she shuddered any time she saw a truck with a skull-and-crossbones decal. It was never him, but it could've been.

The Crab Shack was steady work, which also meant it never changed. Greeting and seating, drinks filled to overflowing, whole forests worth of napkins. Adults wearing bibs. Annie never felt gratitude for the regulars' patronage, not like Phil, who sucked up to them like a blowfish with a faux-hawk, who told everyone they had a beautiful family, even the groups who came in wearing visibly stained clothing and misshapen grins and smacked each other before the fried appetizer course.

None seemed particularly grateful for Annie's contributions to their meal. A smile, a nod. That was about it. She had overheard the Thompsons' bratty little son, barely ten, call her a bleach-blond bimbo. Mrs. Thompson focused closely on her lobster, head tilted as if she were listening to its last words. Annie could guess where he had learned the phrase, which did have a nice alliterative quality.

Also essential: she had gone back to school anyway, and the fear was lessening each day. Tangible items like textbooks and a campus map grounded her, helped her feel connected to the neatly plotted expanse of the quad, where students lingered and chatted with utter ease and belonging. Annie had no time to pause. She was setting her alarm and getting to campus early. She was leaving afterward, back to the Crab Shack.

Her hair, pinned up at the neck, had begun to fall down, and she gathered it back into the clip. Come on. She would not let bleach anywhere near her hair. The box said "Honey Blonde," the brand with the ad declaring "Because you're worth it." For some reason, she wrote this in her notebook.

Phil materialized at her elbow, a crease between his eyes. "Babe, is that homework?"

"Oh, sorry," she stammered, stashing the notebook beneath the reservations. Tonight, there had been none. "It was slow, so I thought . . ."

"Totally slow," he agreed. "Sloth-like. Listen, use my office instead. You can save your work on my computer and at least sit in a comfy chair."

"What about hostessing?"

"Maya can cover. She's been playing Uno with Rafael all night, anyway."

Annie exhaled. "I brought a flash drive," she said. A campus freebie at registration, along with a bright-red stress ball. Phil logged into the computer and left her alone. The chair was very comfortable. Annie's fingers warmed up and flew across the keyboard, her thoughts unlocked. Out of habit, she reached for the middle drawer of Phil's desk and pulled. Locked.

Credit cards maxed out, Annie was careful with her budget, and she had saved for two years to pay for the upcoming semester's tuition, parking pass, lab fees, and textbooks. But she had not accounted for inflation. Textbooks were outrageous now. After rent, payday would not be enough. Did she still need to buy Dr. Lang's anthropology textbook if Dr. Lang was no longer the professor? Lucinda Gregory had mentioned no texts. Anthro could wait. Biology and Interpersonal Communications could not.

Part of her savings came from small amounts taken from the restaurant's petty cash. It was a loan, she told herself. Only she knew the terms of the arrangement. Phil locked the drawer, but she knew he kept the key atop the framed print of an iceberg and a whale. Phil would give her money if she asked. She didn't want to owe him, though in fact she did, now.

These were her essentials. Some of them. And she could not, for the life of her, figure out how to fit them in the form of a question, essential or otherwise. *Jeopardy!* and Alex Trebek sprang to mind: What is being called something you aren't? Who is a woman older than her classmates but not so much older that the campus and/or local newspaper would write a feature about her? Who cannot say her ex-husband's name aloud, for fear of conjuring him?

She was more prone to statements, not questions. She was the type of woman who would unlock a drawer and take what she needed. Books were essential. It was almost noble, she told herself, to steal for essentials.

The next class, Lucinda Gregory met the students in the hall outside the classroom and ushered them to an outdoor courtyard with wrought-iron tables. She shooed away the few people already congregated there, announcing that she had reserved the space. Her wink to Annie indicated this was a lie, but it was a nice day, so Annie kept her mouth shut.

"We'll start with a little light yoga, then head to our new classroom," Lucinda said.

Kyle wore a Pacers jersey with a white T-shirt underneath, stretching his enormous wings to mimic Lucinda's warrior pose. "My coach is gonna love this," he said.

"You play basketball?" Chelsea asked. "Like on our college team?" Now they were pals.

After a ten-minute warmup, Lucinda led the students to the engineering building. Start of semester rejiggering, she said. A larger class needed the old room. This smaller classroom held lab tables. In one corner waited dread-locked Cliff, bright-blue eyes shining. "Surprise," he exclaimed in a soft voice.

Lucinda registered Cliff's presence with wariness, as if she had taken a pull of coffee and found it to be Kool-Aid.

"No worries, I'm here on a pro bono basis," he said.

She ignored him. "I only have a few copies," she announced, passing out papers. "It would seem that my copier code has ceased functionality. A glitch of the modern age. Please share with a partner."

Cliff crossed the room to Annie's seat. "Partner up, yeah?"

Some of Lucinda's copies were stapled upside down, another fault of the copier. The article was about meditation. Learning how to unlock the secrets within your unconscious mind. Deep breathing, attempting peace.

"How is this anthropology?" Chelsea asked.

"Think of this as a prewriting exercise for your papers," Lucinda said. "Deep-six your expectations. Before we can dive into our work, we must dive into ourselves."

Kyle muttered loud enough to be heard: "What the fuck?"

Lucinda offered a wan smile. "We all need to work on ourselves. Some more than others. Read through the steps, and then begin."

"Begin what?" Chelsea was almost vibrating with incredulity.

"Begin meditating, of course," Lucinda said. "I'm going to start right now."

She perched on the desk, cross-legged, and closed her eyes. Nervous laughter erupted. Cliff silenced the class by holding up one hand. "It works," he said. "Just try it."

A few students opted out. Chelsea scribbled notes in her planner: assignments, Pilates, work schedule, all laid out neatly in little calendar boxes. After thirty minutes, Lucinda cleared her throat. Cliff nudged Annie's foot with one combat boot, and she reluctantly opened her eyes. His gaze unsettled her. "You went all the way out there, I could tell," he said.

Lucinda clapped her hands. "Pen and paper time," she said. "Write about what you experienced for your autoethnography. Come to office hours if you want to discuss."

"What if we didn't experience anything?" Chelsea asked. Lucinda either didn't hear, or pretended not to hear.

Annie was fully relaxed; she had never done anything like that before, and while she may not have gone all the way out there, whatever that meant, she had stilled her mind. It felt revolutionary. "You've got to try," she told Chelsea.

Chelsea regarded her older classmate, head tilted, her blowout frizzing. Annie smiled at her. In return, Chelsea leaned forward. She sniffed Annie's hair.

"Girl, you smell like french fries," Chelsea said. "I was hungry the whole class."

The Java Brew House was where Lucinda held office hours: hippie chic with a colorful chalkboard of specials. Behind the counter, Cliff turned on a blender and two industrial-sized coffee bean grinders. A woman holding a sleeping baby glared at him, then resumed describing the benefits of chia seeds to her friend. Annie tiptoed around the baby to Lucinda's round two-top, where books and papers were spread out before her.

"You like this better than an office, huh?" Annie asked.

"Don't have one," Lucinda said, crisp and businesslike. A faint jingle came from her person. "Maybe if I'd been called in earlier, they would've found space for me."

"Did you always want to be a professor?" Annie asked.

"Oh, God, no," she said. "And I'm not really one now. I teach. I'm part-time. Professors . . . do something more important." She waved one hand vaguely. "It's beyond me. I wanted to be an astronaut. Or an archaeologist. That's how I fell in love with anthropology."

Annie's own childhood dreams were to be in commercials, mainly so she could eat unlimited sugared cereal. That, or she wanted to be an Olympic swimmer. Even though, as a fifth grader, she was too nervous to compete at the swim meets she had been training for, causing her parents to decide it was a waste of time and money. Now she needed to get through prereqs before she could apply to the nursing program. Those didn't seem like details worth sharing with her teacher.

"I've been out of school for a while," Annie admitted to Lucinda. "Could you narrow down what you want with this assignment?"

Lucinda squinted at her. "Like a prompt?"

"That would be great, yeah."

Lucinda reached under her scarves and into her blouse, straightening a silver chain with dangling dog tags. "No," she said. "Let your confusion be your guide. You are the subject of your cultural study, and the approach for the autoethnography is yours. Figuring it out is part of the work."

"But I'm not ethnic," Annie said, just as Cliff brought over a green smoothie and a latte that neither had ordered. Annie went beet red. Cliff could pass for "a white man with a tan," as Jackson would describe himself during summer construction season, his skin bronzed and branded with extreme tan lines that never faded. Annie's mother would've called Cliff "a mix." Her father would've used other words, which Annie knew better than to say out loud.

"No offense," she said quickly. Cliff's impassive face made her stomach drop.

"Hey, you can't help your pigment situation," he said, then burst out laughing. He handed her the latte, which she gratefully accepted. "Taste-test this for me."

He gestured to the open notebook on Annie's lap. "Life is a blank slate, no?"

"My background is white," Annie said, as if to apologize. "Basically blank." She sounded like Jackson, forcing a classification where none was required.

"So, European and whatnot," Cliff said. "Like Ms. Lucinda and her kin."

Lucinda and Cliff locked eyes in some understanding that shut out the world, that shut Annie out, embarrassing her. Annie stared at her notebook.

"Remember my first paper for you?" Cliff asked Lucinda, and she pursed her lips before sipping the smoothie. It looked like a weedy lawn.

"Not now," Lucinda murmured.

"I wrote an ode," he told Annie.

"Cliff," Lucinda warned.

Annie checked her watch. She still needed to change her clothes before her shift. The answer for her paper was that she wasn't going to get an answer.

"My essay was about admiration," he said. "Whatever you write, Annie, will be totally unique and cool. I wouldn't stress."

Annie smiled. "When did you graduate, Cliff?"

"Future tense: when *will* I graduate?" he said. "My victory lap's gone on for a minute. Lucinda can tell you."

Lucinda pointedly waved goodbye to Cliff. "Nobody's a blank," she told Annie. "Everybody comes from somewhere. A culture, a group, something larger than yourself. Write about that. I bet you'll have lots to say about your life." Her eyes trailed Cliff back to the counter. The dog tags jingled.

"I'll try," Annie said. "Are those yours?"

"They belong to my departed," Lucinda said. Her expression was inscrutable.

"God, I'm so sorry," Annie said. "Iraq or Afghanistan?"

Lucinda focused on Annie again. "What? No. We broke up. It was for the best. And I got to keep these." She clinked them together between thumb and forefinger and winked at Annie.

Later, when Annie saw Cliff leaving an American Sign Language class, she asked him about his autoethnography.

"Ethnos," he said. "From the Greek. Folk, people, nation!"

"I'm not Greek, either," she tried to joke, but he didn't seem to hear. "I mean, what did you write about?"

Some of his classmates were leaving the room. They signed parting sentiments, laughing silently. Cliff joined in. Annie understood none of it. She was fascinated. Maybe she would register for ASL in the spring semester. If the Crab Shack had a Deaf customer, she could greet them in their language, actually have a conversation. What if the ones who pointed to their orders on the menu were Deaf? She hadn't considered that before.

Cliff continued talking with his hands. "Kind of a tribute, I guess you'd call it."

"Sorry, how's that an ethnography?" she asked.

"Yeah, no," he said, turning back to her, tapping two fingers against thumb with an exaggerated frown. "It wasn't. I got points for creativity, though. And probably flattery."

With no computer at home, Annie's flash drive stayed tucked in her backpack. She wrote by hand, continuing the work she had started in Phil's office, where she had unlocked the desk drawer and taken five twenties, enough for her remaining textbooks. He checked in on her twice, and the second time there was a look on his face that made her wonder: had he seen her, somehow? Or heard the metal drawer opening and closing? Did he have a hidden camera, or was he purposely setting her up to find out who had taken the money? Phil did not keep good track of finances. She saw him stuff crumpled wads of bills into the manila envelope. For all she knew, he was using that cash for his own purposes. Maybe underreporting the books, fudging the margins. It didn't take an Intro Psych course: she suspected Phil because she felt guilty. She would pay the money back in time.

She filled the bathtub with nearly scalding water and a heavy pour of lavender bubble bath, balancing her notebook and pen on the tub's edge. She was free-associating about Jackson and his meanness, and the way her mother looked at her when she dropped out of school: without the slightest hint of surprise. Pretty much everyone in their family had dropped out at some point. They failed. Her mother gave her a similar look when she announced she was getting a divorce. Her mother loved Jackson and his Tom Cruise jawline, and so had Annie. His looks and charm fooled everyone. Her mother said that she was overreacting, the time that Jackson put Annie in a headlock at a cousin's pool party and dunked her repeatedly. Turning her hair to seaweed. "You can't take a joke!" they all said, when Annie stormed off wrapped in the faded red towel with hibiscus print.

The same towel she took to Florida when the divorce was finalized. She put Disney World on her new Visa, and ate alone at the German biergarten in Epcot Center. Meant to be liberating, it was the loneliest five days of her life. She tried to make conversation with the Spanish-speaking maids at her hotel, minutes outside the Magic Kingdom but hundreds of dollars cheaper. None of the maids had been to Disney World. "Sabes Mickey y Pluto?" Annie had asked, her limited Spanish like a low-budget educational children's television show. "Sí, claro," the maids acknowledged, smiling, but there the conversation stopped. Now, after a week of college-level

Spanish, she could have talked about the weather. Offered an orange. Or they could've sat together on the back lot's concrete parking bumpers, commiserating and smoking cigarettes.

The back stoop. Where her parents sat her and her little brother Donny when they locked them out of the house. Annie understood by age six. They were either fighting or screwing, maybe both, and Annie kept her hands over Donny's ears. Annie heard everything. After, they would unlock the door but wouldn't open it. Annie knew to wait not only for the click of the turning lock, but the footsteps retreating.

Once, Jackson had locked her out in winter while she was wearing only a bathrobe. She could hear the crystals forming in her wet hair, fresh from the shower, crackling pieces of ice scented like freesia shampoo. She shivered, too proud to go to a neighbor's door. They did not know any of their neighbors. She shivered now, in the hot bath. Stupid white trash, Jackson had said from inside. Why do I bother with such a piece of shit? Tell me you're done lying and I'll open the door.

She swore that she hadn't lied when he asked who had come over while he bartended at his second job. She was alone the whole time. But that day she became a liar because she wanted back inside and it was easier than trying to convince a man who would not be convinced.

"I'm done," she had said, as quietly as she could, mouthing the words in the dark sliver where Jackson had parted the blinds. His face had brightened; his lip curled. I knew it, he had said. The lock turning, the door opening, to inside where it was warm, where Jackson did what he did to her and it was somehow her fault. Because I love you so much, he would say, tearful. And she believed it. His tenderness in those moments convinced her. Desire filled her. They would make up, everything fine between them for weeks, even a month. Until he would turn on her. No one knew. Not her mother, not Phil.

Soon, Lucinda Gregory would know. Annie was writing the story down, planning to share it with a teacher who was practically a stranger. Was this an autoethnography? She wasn't sure. She dropped the notebook onto the bath mat and dunked her entire head beneath the soapy water. Stayed there until she couldn't any longer. Bubbles climbed up her nasal passages, and she emerged, sputtering. She had at least one more page to write.

Annie arrived early to campus so she could type and print the paper. Rather than pack her work clothes, she was wearing them: a gauzy blouse and tight black pants that needed to be washed, chunky red lacquered jewelry, gold espadrilles. Girl, she did smell like french fries. In the computer lab she checked her email and found a personal message from the registrar.

Annie's anthropology professor, the email stated, was not Lucinda Gregory, but Dr. Lang. Her "new" classroom was the one Lucinda made them vacate after the first day. Reenrollment in a different section was an option. It was early in the semester; accommodations would be made. The registrar closed with a kicker: *Lucinda Gregory is no longer employed by this University; we suggest you end or avoid all communication with her.*

Annie replied at once: *Why fire somebody in the middle of the semester? Is Lucinda Gregory OK? What happened to her?*

The response arrived in minutes. *I am not at liberty to discuss personnel (or former personnel) matters, but rest assured that Ms. Gregory appears to be fine. She was never officially hired to teach your section. The University and I once again apologize for this complicated situation, and wish you the best of luck.*

Annie blew out a long breath she didn't know she had been holding. She wanted her professor, fake or not, to read her work. She wanted credit for having done this difficult task. She saved and printed a copy, tucking the pages into her bag.

An email from Cliff materialized on the screen; she opened it by clicking the mouse like a game show buzzer. He asked how many semesters she had left, as he was nearly finished through the GI Bill. And what were her thoughts on Italian films? The campus film festival was coming up. "Mayhaps you'd like to join me," he wrote. His autoethnography was attached in case a model would be useful. She read his paper, heat rising in her cheeks at the erotic allusions to an unnamed mentor, a statuesque woman who wore her beloved's dog tags, naked, in bed.

Annie trekked to the far-flung engineering building at class time to see if Lucinda might have come to say goodbye. Two students who hadn't checked their messages were the only ones there: Kyle and a petite girl who had never spoken. Wherever Chelsea was, no doubt she had taken action. Annie gave them the lowdown, and Kyle lowered his forehead to the desk and gave three quick taps.

"What a pain," he said. "But there's no class today, so that's a plus."

"I mean, there is, but with a different professor in another building," Annie said. "I'm heading there now if you want to come."

Kyle smiled, the picture of innocence. "Yeah, I didn't see the email," he said.

The petite girl spoke for the first time on her way out the door: "It's been real," she deadpanned.

Annie hustled across campus and climbed the stairs to the old anthropology classroom. In the vestibule, Lucinda sat alone at a study table. She saw Annie immediately. "I was hoping we'd cross paths," she said.

Annie slowed down. "Are you OK? What happened?"

Lucinda rewrapped the purple scarf around her neck with a flick. "They asked me to teach the course," she said. "Back in the spring. I'd planned on the income. Enrollment was low, so they gave my section to one of the full-timers, Jenny Lang. Who then wants me to cover for her so she can give a talk. She didn't offer to pay me. Put it on your CV, said Jenny. Well, I'd do it for free. I *am* doing it for free. Actually, I paid for parking to teach this class."

"I'm sorry," Annie said. "You should talk to your boss. Um, your old boss?"

Lucinda waved her off. "He's useless. And Jenny Lang's not speaking to me at the moment, understandably. She used to be part-time, too, and has since risen in the ranks and esteem of our glorious institution. Not mental; I shouldn't have joked. She's off presenting conference papers. Whereas I prefer working with students, and being a student of life. And, so."

Annie wasn't sure what to say. The silence hung over them for a thick moment until Lucinda clapped twice, clearing her air. "Your autoethnography. Have you written it? Are you ready for me to read it?"

This wouldn't count; Lucinda Gregory wasn't her teacher anymore. Annie paused. She wanted to ask about Cliff, and his "tribute" to his teacher. Had Lucinda gotten in trouble for dating a student? She wanted to ask, What's his story, anyway? And why had Cliff mentioned your kin's ethnicity? Had they disapproved of him, or the relationship? She kept her questions to herself. She and Phil were still together, at least technically, for now. And Dr. Lang's class could wait a little longer. Annie took the neatly stapled pages from her backpack, where the appetizer coupons for the Crab Shack remained. She gave the whole stack to her teacher. "From my restaurant," she said, with a kind of apologetic pride.

"Thank you, how thoughtful!" Lucinda said. "I will use them posthaste. Take a stroll and give me twenty minutes. Then we'll talk."

"All right," Annie said. She scuffed the hallway in her gold espadrilles, glad she was not watching Lucinda read her paper about Jackson. The years she endured, scars inside and out, hidden in her mind's closet. Writing the paper unlocked the door. She had thought she would be more scared about what would emerge from that dark interior. Instead the story turned factual, black ink on white paper, like some distant historical past. She used to think that artifacts just *were*, a collection of things dug up and dusted off, but it turned out you could make them yourself. In an hour, Lucinda's feedback would be an artifact. Her class already was archived. Within months, the semester would be over, and Annie would be looking back on this moment as . . . what? She didn't know yet. Mentally, she calculated how many paydays until she could repay her debt. Then she would start fresh, find a new job, break it off with Phil, whose kindness did not make up for absent spark. He deserved better than what she gave, and what she took.

Annie took a long drink at the fountain and resumed walking the halls. She passed the open door of an ASL class where the words I LOVE YOU were red-markered on the whiteboard, inside a crookedly-drawn heart. The students signed in unison: I love you, I love you, I love you. Cliff stood at the front of the room, demonstrating, his classmates' faces rapt. Maybe they saw Annie standing there and maybe they didn't. Mayhaps. She felt like an intruder, but she couldn't turn away. I love you, they repeated with their hands.

She was not their subject; still, a wave of feeling washed over her. You, in the hall, European and whatnot. You survived to tell the tale. To share your story so someone else could hold it for you. Only seven minutes had passed. She crept around the corner to peek at Lucinda. Annie's paper was on her lap; she scribbled longhand notes across the page. Chin atop fist, she shook her head and wiped away tears. Annie slipped around the corner and leaned her forehead against the cool glass case that held a coiled emergency fire-hose. Witnessing Lucinda's reaction loosened a tightness around her ribs: Yes. What happened had been that bad. All the signs Annie had missed or ignored. It's because I love you so much, Jackson would say, cradling her narrow shoulders, mindful to avoid the bruises in the shape of his fingers. I love you, too, she would say. They had meant it. They were lying.

She could practice saying it true. Alone in the hallway, she repeated the motions the ASL class made, watching her hands move in the reflection of the glass case. The signs weren't hard to learn, once you knew them. Two fists crossboned over the heart, then an escaped pointer finger, singling out the beloved, you, I love you, imagine your life like this, where words disappear, become action.

Hysterectomy

The whale-colored sky is giving me that Syracuse feeling again. Swollen clouds inch downward, nearly kissing the piles of dingy snow already on the ground, and the high-pressure system traps me somewhere in between. Like the sky's squeezing my lungs. My Corolla skids a little on the salted beltway, and I slow down and attempt even breaths, cursing the cold air still spewing from the vents. I started the car twenty minutes ago back in the parking lot. This was after the doctor told me he wanted to remove my uterus and I punched a pregnant woman in the stomach.

I don't know how she's doing. I didn't stick around to ask. Instead I sped off, thinking about the doctor, who wore an orange-and-blue striped tie. Syracuse colors. I remembered reading a study about germs being carried on doctors' neckties.

He had said maybe it was mercury from the lake, which was back in the news. Eat any Onondaga Lake bluegills lately? He was teasing, this man who recommended I schedule an appointment so he could remove my womb. The lake was still frozen but a study just came out saying it was okay to eat the fish again after a forty-year ban. People won't even swim in that lake, but now they can eat its fish. But only one or two per year, and not if you're pregnant.

I'm not pregnant. After the procedure, I will never be pregnant. I am a nonsmoker/light drinker who pours soy milk on cereal and eats green salads for lunch. I had only gone in because of the bleeding, and also the intermittent twitch, not a big deal, in fact I felt foolish calling to schedule the appointment. The doctor described my growths with multisyllable words. He opened and closed his hands, showing approximate measurements. Left untreated, he called my uterus names like Possible Cancer Risk. I only heard about half of his words. I keep expecting him to call. My cell phone has been quiet so far. Maybe I put my number on the form. Maybe not. The only missed call is from Roger Wilco. He didn't leave a message and I don't call him back.

I am told that my age—thirty-three—is an issue. The ticktocking time bomb of questions winds me more than any body clock. Why aren't you married yet? Don't you think that maybe—now, don't get mad—it's because you're the teensiest bit cold with men? Isn't that the cutest baby? God, don't those rolls of fat make you want one, too?

My cousins, older than me but not by that much, are marrying off their own children. At the weddings of my baby-faced second cousins, I sit with the other single misfits. I fly home in the summer to the swirling pollen of Illinois for this special torture. There are multiple tables of us, but we never manage to pair off, to follow up with phone calls; often we don't bother to speak. All we have in common are sparse grocery lists. We shop for too much or not enough. In our refrigerators, head lettuce and celery bunches fill the crisper drawer. The vegetables, more than a single person can eat, wilt and spoil.

The snow comes down lightly. It's snowed every day for the last month—not even a record. I've gotten used to the snowflakes on my windshield and in my eyes the same way I've gotten used to TV static after the free cable was discovered and cut off. Today I was supposed to design a three-color bro-chure, eat my chicken salad sandwich for lunch, go to the doctor, and return to work. Tonight I had planned to watch *Spellbound* on Channel 7. I don't think I can sit still for Hitchcock.

Any other day, you would be right to blame me for hitting a pregnant woman in her belly. But today I think I should get a pass. At least we were still at the doctor's. She could have gone back inside.

Before our appointments, we had sat across from each other in the wait-ing room. I'd just arrived. She shifted her weight like she had been there awhile. She wore a green scrub uniform with her blond likeness smiling from the picture ID clipped to it, and a long cardigan sweater with fake fur around the collar. No coat, despite the snow and the twenty-three degree temperature. On her lap sat a workbook: "Your Whole Pregnancy." She smiled broadly, revealing sharp, white teeth.

"If they don't come get us soon, what do you say we bust down the door?" she said. Glittery stickers on her ID badge spelled G-A-I-L.

I smiled, surprised. I've lived in Syracuse a long time, and people rarely struck up conversations. They would help you shovel your car out, but grunt and avoid eye contact when you tried to thank them. It had to be the weather: everybody all hunched up and unrecognizable in down parkas, rushing to heated buildings and cars. Except they acted that way in summer, too, minus parkas. My own coat, black-down-filled with a puffy hood, sat on the chair next to me, occupying as much space as a small child.

"When are you due?" I asked Gail, a safe question.

"Three weeks to go." She splayed her unpolished, bitten fingernails across her stomach and drummed lightly. "I can't wait to meet the little guy. Want to see him?"

She was peppy, the cheerleader type, and it wouldn't have shocked me if she had spread her legs right there to display her centimeters of dilation. Instead she pulled an ultrasound picture from her purse and handed it to me.

I cooed. The black-and-white image looked spookily beautiful. A lovely little alien, celestial and floating, perhaps sucking his thumb. My belly twinged as it had for the past two months. Sometimes it hurt but not right now. This week I had been bleeding again—off schedule.

"And there's his wee-wee." Gail pointed with the fingernail of her pinky finger, which she then held up and wiggled. I had to laugh. A nurse called Gail's name, and she rose with great effort. Gail was short, and her belly stuck out and up, pushing at her green scrubs. Her stomach was so perfectly round, she looked like she was wearing one of those false-pregnancy vests. Her breasts seemed to weigh her down. She caught me staring.

"I know," she said. "Mother Nature is ridiculous, isn't she?"

"I suppose I'll look like that soon," I offered. I don't know why I said it. I wasn't pregnant. I wasn't even sleeping with anyone. Last week I had let Roger Wilco kiss me in his car after dinner, but that was all. I was taller than Gail, on the skinny side, and in my tight jeans I did not look the least bit pregnant. I should have kept my coat on. The thought crept in: What would my breasts and belly look like, *feel* like, if I were as far along as Gail? I smiled despite myself. I picked at a lock of my reddish-brown hair and twisted it around one finger.

Gail broke into a huge grin that bordered on parental pride. "Well, congratulations." Her eyes flicked from my face to my flat belly. "Here I've been gabbing and didn't even ask about you. Which kind of prenatal vitamins do you take?"

M y apartment is two exits down the beltway, but I'm not ready to go there. When the sign for campus appears, I chop down on the turn signal. She wants to know about me? I don't take vitamins. I've never taken a sick day in my life. Not in school, not at work. I schedule my illnesses. Time to break the streak; three-color brochures seem more meaningless than they were before. The day's almost over, besides.

Up the hill and under low clouds: the gray languages building rumored to be haunted. A castle, a fortress. Some said it was the model for a house on TV—*The Addams Family? The Munsters?* I can't remember.

My sophomore year Spanish class was on the third floor. Once I tried to tell Profesór Stephens that I was too embarrassed to speak in front of the class. *Estoy embarazada,* I said. He explained the words meant "I'm pregnant." But I wasn't. Not yet.

My stomach gurgles, craving sweets. The bakery on Genesee makes the best half-moon cookies in town. Instead of taking the shortcut, I zigzag five blocks of one-way streets, slowing for pedestrians, no, protestors, at the Planned Parenthood clinic.

Two elderly men shuffle along the icy sidewalk with their signs: GOD IS CRYING and IT IS A CHILD, IT IS NOT A CHOICE. I'm bothered by the lack of contractions. This is where I had it done, spring break of my junior year. The protesters must have been on vacation then. I went out with Ty for five months, and he was in Huntington Beach the day of my appointment— We're broken up, he pointed out when I'd called the week before to ask for a ride. He dumped me for refusing to abort our child, and then I went and did it anyway. Do I wish I hadn't done it? Yes. Do I wish to be a single mother, with a child who would now be twelve years old? I do not. A twelve-year-old would abandon you as soon as she could. Enlist in a small army of friends, uniformed in half-shirts and tight jeans like pop stars.

But a baby. A pink-swaddled mass of sweet breath and tender skin. A concave chest scented with Baby Magic lotion. I can't think about a baby.

I remember waiting in the stirrups for the vacuum. An infant's faint cry drifted from the hallway through the door, hiccupy and small. I couldn't tell if I was imagining it. I bit back tears. Repeated in my head, *You wanted this.*

I drove home hunched over my abdomen, and spent the next three days with cramping, curled on the blue plaid couch in front of daytime television. On the fourth day I finished my midterm computer design project. My roommate came back with a tan and a fondness for strawberry daiquiris and the semester went on.

I slow the car and roll down the window. A blast of lake-effect storm air sweeps into the car. One of the protesters sees me and takes a tentative step toward the street. He's wearing a tan overcoat, too lightweight for this weather, and leather gloves. He looks like a retired lawyer or professor.

"We don't all have choices," I yell.

"We do." He frowns. He has the same baby-fine white hair my grandfather had. Downy, like a chick's. "Each of us can make a positive decision for a positive outcome."

"Not today, buddy," I say to the old man. "Not today." He looks at me as if he understands something I don't.

No one but Ty knew I was pregnant. Not my family, not my roommate. I've told a few people, since. An ex-boyfriend. An ex-therapist. Nobody recent. I roll up the automatic window with jerky stabs and shut the protester out. I floor the accelerator and run a yellow light, but nobody hits me.

At the bakery I grab three half-pints of whole milk from the case and order half a dozen large, cakey cookies. Each is perfectly round, iced with thick chocolate and white frosting. Half-moons for a woman whose parts will be divided from the whole. The cashier, the one with the gray hair, gives me the same toothy, pleasant smile Gail did earlier. I start to glower, but then I say: "I think I'm pregnant," and I feel a little better. The cashier's name is Wilma. She never remembers me.

Her eyes open wide. "Wonderful!" She reaches up for the dangling piece of string hanging from the ceiling dispenser, and wraps it around the white bakery box with a flourish. She snips the string and the other end rises gently toward the dispenser. Behind her on the metal counter, bread dough waiting to be punched down rises above the edge of a huge metal bowl.

"You say you think you're pregnant?" She points to a framed picture on the wall. Three girls and a boy in 1970s-era clothing—corduroy pants, printed rayon shirts—sit on a fake wooden fence in front of a photography studio's fake nature backdrop. A black-and-white ultrasound picture is tucked into the picture frame. Two fetuses are visible.

"They'll be my first grandkids." Wilma's chin juts out, proudly protective. She sees my expression and her smile fades. Her eyebrows knit together, twin question marks drawn in eyebrow pencil. I don't know what my face looks like. For a brief moment, I wish I could see what she sees. I seize my box and paper sack of milk cartons without a word and turn on my heel. Two of the six cookies in the box are broken. I sit in my old Corolla and eat every crumb, washing down the bigger chunks with milk.

I should go home. My apartment is on the other side of campus. My pants feel tight from the sweets and sloshing milk, added pressure in my belly. I get stuck at the stoplight on Adams, the steep hill by the hospital. A terrible place to drive a stick shift. The snow has stopped but the pavement wears a coat of ice. I press down hard on the brake even though the car isn't moving. The 1960s-era hospital, boxy and utilitarian, displays its name in raised sans-serif letters. When the light turns green I could slide backwards, wheels spinning, and crash into the green Cadillac behind me. I could over-accelerate and rear-end the white ladder truck ahead. I could freeze here. In the rearview mirror, I notice a streak of white frosting in my hair. With my tongue, I grab the strand in my mouth and suck. When the light turns green my foot is still jammed on the brake. The Cadillac driver honks. My cell phone rings. I scramble for the clutch and gear, rattled to the point of screaming. But that's not me. I carry these screams around, lodged in my throat. I swallow, remain silent, refusing to bear witness to myself.

There's a bank parking lot near the university village. My car rolls over noisy layers of impacted snow and slush, snow and slush, the crust of this city's earth. The phone continues its high-pitched wail in pulsing intervals. It could only be the doctor or police. I stumble from the car, eyeing the bank of plowed snow huddled against the bank's brick wall. My underhand lob sends the phone into the snow pile, where it sinks with a swish. It glows faintly, blue inside the exhaust-soaked snow.

My ears and head are buzzing; my hands have gone numb. The cold air and the relief of phonelessness shush me; the sloping sidewalk invites a stroll. It's close to dinnertime and on the hill I can see the glow of the Dome, a lacrosse game going on inside. I picture the doctor sitting five rows from the field, having forgotten me and Gail and women problems.

Then the twitch is back. My uterus wants attention, bad. It says, Remember me? You've ignored me for so long. Every month since you were thirteen, I've given you everything I had. Now I'm all used up. I'm done. This bleeding? It's a last blast. Ha ha.

I can ignore you even longer, I tell it. A panhandler in a plaid flannel work coat standing outside 'Cuse Convenience cries out to me. I had spoken out loud. He steps up his hustle. He shakes his red plastic change cup. It's the kind the college students use at keg parties and discard all over the street and yards, dots that show You (Were) Here.

"Don't ignore me, baby," he says. "We'd make a good couple. You kinda cute."

"Kinda?" I snarl over my shoulder.

He says something else, but I'm out of range. Through the windows of the bar where Ty and I met, I see lazy beginnings of other people's evenings: a group of three pink-faced girls with highlighted hair, like models in a Coke commercial, bubbly and shiny and not yet drunk. Two guys with wet-gelled hair and faded jeans talk closely at the bar—maybe a couple. Ty and I used to sit on those high black barstools, leaning into each other. The place is packed, even though it's early on a Wednesday. Is there a version of me and Ty inside? I can picture one -half of the couple, the guppy-faced girl, drunk and gullible. Oh, that girl, I shudder at what she didn't know, the rotting sugarplum visions that filled her head. That marriage was a vague dress. That babies were tickets redeemable for club membership. That the future meant another person, a blank face sketched with the features of whoever was near. That she was me, and I wish she would learn something, fast.

If the idea of entering the bar didn't repulse me, I would search faces until I found the closest version. Tell her, *Go. Now.* Instead I pace up and down the sidewalk, by the shop windows displaying batik dresses, gold-plated pot bowls, picture menus of Korean food. I pretend not to notice the police cruiser parked in front of the ice cream shop. I didn't hit her that hard, I want to say, though I doubt they want me to say anything at all.

For a minute the village felt like a place where I could be unseen. But it's never been that place. I don't fit here, then or now. I shouldn't have come. I slide around the corner, retreating from the police car.

My cell phone remains where I chucked it. I dig in the dirty snow and press the right buttons, placing the cold phone against my ear. The single message on my voice mail is from Roger Wilco, the married college professor who has taken me out to dinner. Twice. Relief and disappointment flood me. I met him a couple months ago when I called to discuss his book jacket, which I was designing. My company contracts with the university press. He had written a book about mating rituals among lower-order mammals. Parts were funny; I had told him so. He told me how pleased he was that I *got* it. Most people, he said, simply *don't*. Roger Wilco isn't his real name, and he doesn't know I call him that in my head. I haven't told anyone about him. Who would I tell? Maggie would advise me to cut it off—*He's married*, I can hear her say. She and her husband, Andrew, both work in my office. They've never invited me to their home for dinner, yet they're interested in my paltry love life. They dole out advice like pity on a cracker. I relish keeping Roger Wilco secret. His first name really is Roger. Each time we had met, he wore collared shirts under sweaters and stiff, dark jeans. He was clean-shaven, though a beard would look nice on him. His message said he would like to see me again. He wondered if he could take me to dinner. Tonight. His voice was silky and professional.

"What did the shrew say to the bat?" he asked. "Call me to find out."

I do not want punch lines. I do not want additional information about mammals. I do not want to be the kind of woman who has nothing better to do than accept a date for the same night. But I do want the distraction of dinner and company, even if it's with a married man who glances over his shoulder twice before the salads are served. Both times we went out, I convinced myself it wasn't a date. Two professionals, one a little lonely, sharing a meal. Then last time he kissed me. I reminded him he was married and told him I was Not That Kind of Person. Then I kissed him, blushed, and jumped out of the car. Which was Not Like Me.

I drive with one hand on my belly. My uterus deserves a second opinion. I know it won't get one. I can't bear to hear for a second time what I already know is true. My midsection twinges, as if to say: trust your gut.

The doctor had talked at me quickly, glancing over the sheaf of forms about the procedure. He checked his watch and advised me to search online to learn more about elective hysterectomy. I was still sitting on the examining table, pantsless.

"Do you know the etymology of the word." He asked questions without question marks. "They used to think taking out the uterus would cure hysteria in women."

"And does that work." I imitated his inflection.

He scratched behind his ear and mussed his graying hair. "Well. I think we both know today it's a health issue. Preventing future problems—cancer for one. It's about your comfort and health, right." Another non-question.

Syracuse men's basketball and lacrosse posters hung on his office wall, and I stared at the players—local celebrities—who looked vaguely familiar. He was waiting for me to get up and leave. If I didn't, he would. Tickets to tonight's game protruded from his breast pocket, beside the germy orange-and-blue tie.

"Language," he said. He headed to the door and slapped his clipboard like a coach. My paperwork fluttered slightly. "It's pretty darn interesting."

After he had directed me to the waiting room to schedule the procedure, I took the appointment card from the receptionist and trudged to my car. I hunched over the steering wheel with my red leather purse on my lap. I had made an appointment, not a decision, yet things seemed decided. No children, no grandchildren to give my parents, who had practically given up on me anyway. I couldn't bear seeing my mother's pure, beaming face whenever she held a baby, followed by a rueful look in my direction. I thought of Ty, a casual college boyfriend, who wasn't supposed to remain in my head. Most of my memories of him are of sex, gritty sheets. I cannot conjure his face, just the outline, the shock of blond hair across his forehead, a mouth like a slash that bled words. The pre-op instructions were wadded inside my purse. My mother would want to know, the whole state of Illinois would want to know. But I couldn't call—not yet. My cousins and second cousins made routine "I'm pregnant" phone calls across the country. What would my call announce? "This morning I was a whole person. Now I am _____."

Gail had walked out of the office, a black canvas bag hanging from her arm. She was eating a banana. One hand rested on her big belly, swollen like bread dough. She saw me and waved. When I didn't move, she lumbered over to the car. I rolled down the window.

"Hey," she said, "is everything all right?"

It was maybe twenty-five degrees, but she wore only that long furry sweater. Her gold wedding and engagement rings dangled from a chain around her neck.

"Where's your coat?"

"I'm a furnace," she said. "Can't wear one. I'm too big, besides."

Her belly hung suspended at my eye level. She noticed and dropped her head down to the open window. "Do you need to talk?" she asked. She seemed so earnest. At that moment, I loved her for it.

"I'd like that," I said. "Get in."

Now Roger Wilco and I are led to a booth at the window of one of the mall restaurants, three stories up and with a view of the long, skinny lake. Nighttime. Lights reflect in the water. The refinery and alloy process plant, the big pollutants, ring the opposite shore in spitting distance from the fainter lights of ramshackle wooden houses. Those who were too poor to move after the contamination stuck it out for years. Many of them have died of cancer, one newspaper article said. Those who remain can eat the fish again.

Roger wears a black blazer with his dark jeans and a white button-down. He teaches on Wednesdays, which I know from looking up his schedule online.

"So good to see you again," he says, kissing me on the cheek once the young waitress disappears. He pretends we are colleagues. It's for the sake of his wife, the Goya scholar, even though she's lecturing at Columbia this week. By the way he looks at me, I get the feeling he wants in my pants.

In a nearby booth, a pregnant blond woman sits with her young son. She looks like a worn-out Gail. The redheaded toddler next to her places his freckled hand on her arm. "Mom," he says. "How many fish live in the lake?"

She strokes his arm absently, reading her menu. "Lots, baby."

He preens like a cat being petted; I can almost hear him purr. "A million?" The mother doesn't answer. Her blond hair has dark roots, almost black. "A zillion?"

She shakes her head, glances down at him. "Probably not a zillion. Ask Daddy." A bald guy with a goatee sits across from them. He leans over to give his wife and child a kiss. The toddler smacks his lips, *mwah*. The father returns the kiss: *mwah, mwah.*

Roger Wilco sees me watching, gives a cursory smile. "I did the most fascinating research today," he says.

"Better than the book?"

Irritation briefly creases his forehead. "Well. I wouldn't say better. I'd say different. Fascinating in a different way."

I fiddle with my bundled silverware in its white paper napkin and green paper napkin ring. "How was it fascinating?" I try again, and he lights up. He is talking about the tilt of the pelvic floor in certain small mammals. Sperm gets blocked or hits the bull's-eye based on that tilt, a millimeter of difference. At one point, he raises an eyebrow as if to highlight the sexy mystery of mammals. I listen in the way the doctor listened.

Our food arrives. He has the salmon; I have a cheeseburger and fries.

"You're quiet," he says, observing me. He cocks his head to the side. "Usually you're full of bon mots from work. I hope I didn't offend you? In the car last week?"

I pick up a french fry and squash it between my finger and thumb, then put the pulpy mess back on the plate. My body operates on its own: shake head, smile, let him think what he wants. Roger Wilco gives the food and then me a satisfied once-over.

"Good. Well." He smooths the paper napkin on his lap, cuts the salmon into tiny pieces before taking a bite. "What was your day like?"

My mouth doesn't hesitate. "It was violent," I say. "A little bloody. There was bingeing. No purging, though."

He smiles faintly, trying to decide if I'm joking. But his eyes become guarded, watchful, and I can see in his face he is judging my worth: what's inside my pants versus what's inside my head. Both are filled with voltage. His gold wedding band gleams across the table. His art history professor wife is one of the youngest Goya experts in the nation. We did her last book jacket, though I didn't design it. He's never mentioned her to me. I looked her up in our catalog, examining the picture on the back flap. Striking, dark hair, prominent facial bones, full lips. Her bio mentions no children.

When he bursts out laughing, I know I am winning. My pants, my head, it doesn't matter. It's the voltage that matters. He hasn't revealed what the shrew said to the bat. I don't want to know.

"Unpredictable," he says. "I never know what's going to come out of your mouth."

"Me either," I say, and for once today I've told the truth.

Roger Wilco strolls around my apartment as if it were a museum gallery. Hands clasped behind his back, he studies the poster from the Warhol exhibit in Chicago and photographs of my family back in lush and verdant Illinois. He reads the spines of the books in the oak shelf, thumbing my complete Shakespeare. He examines my refrigerator door, with its short phone list and collection of pizza and Thai takeout menus. I could offer him a beer, but opening the fridge would expose decaying vegetables, leftovers in cardboard boxes, sticky, months-old globs of strawberry jam on the top shelf. I have not checked the answering machine, which is in the bedroom. We have not gotten to that part of the tour.

"So," he says, his back to me, prying off a Niagara Falls magnet, cartoon froth and rainbows. I am tired of this pretense, ritual, whatever it is. My mind wants to be separate from the rest of me, switched off. Slowly I lean forward, wrapping my arms around his chest, and though he is bigger than me he loses his balance. He stumbles toward the fridge until I break our fall by putting the flat of my palm on the door. Neither of us moves. I feel as if whatever happens next will sum up my life. My arm shakes a little and bends. The back of his neck is boyish and clean. He has a cowlick and smells of recently-applied aftershave.

"So," I say finally, and kiss the bare skin just under his hairline, where his barber crops close with the clippers.

"This could be a bad idea," he says to my refrigerator door.

A half-hearted refusal, the obvious thing to say. I say nothing. He turns around and kisses me, tasting like salmon and dill sauce. We kiss for a while. It's fine, it's nice. His hands are on my hips, and he's pulling my black sweater over my head. My arms go up like a child being undressed. He is older but not by that much. With my eyes closed, his wedding ring isn't even there.

I have on my black lace bra, lightly padded, because of the doctor visit. Not for the doctor specifically. Because someone—anyone—was going to see me without my clothes. Soon the bra is on the hardwood kitchen floor, then I am. The bra makes an insufficient mattress for the both of us.

"I don't have a condom," he whispers, stopping to look me in the face. His face shows me he does not want to stop. Sweet man, with his mammal research and his art scholar wife, willing to believe—correctly—that I will not infect him with something.

"I'm on the pill," I lie.

The last time I had unprotected sex was in college, with Ty, hulk boy with floppy blond hair who said *Just get an abortion*, casually, as though I had asked him what kind of pizza I should order from Archie's. Roger smiles and leans over me. In my small bathroom's medicine cabinet, there are condoms, no doubt expired.

Roger is doing it to me more than with me, it's fine, it's nice, and my mind refuses to blank the way sex can make it blank, and I'm thinking *pelvic floor, pelvic floor, pelvic floor*. My bare ass and back rub along the dusty old hardwood planks, and I know—I feel—what Roger means when he talks about mammals. I tilt.

Shortly after we finish, when he's still breathing heavy and slowing inside of me, my cell phone sounds a muffled ring from the cave of my purse.

"Who on Earth?" I say to no one in particular.

Back in the doctor's parking lot, Gail and I had sat in the car and I told her what happened. I told her a version of what happened. I told her about the doctor and the fish joke, that my insides had problems and needed to be taken out.

"Oh God," she said. She still didn't know my name. "What about your baby?"

I shrugged, unsure what to do with the lie. "It's probably already gone."

Gail searched my face for a moment, her mouth opening and closing as if in silent prayer. She began to cry. Soon she was gasping for air, hysterical, her face wadded up and used-looking. She couldn't speak.

"Gail," I said. "It's going to be all right. Gail."

A part of me felt put out having to comfort her. I was the one who needed comfort. Her face was in her hands now, and she was as doubled over as she could get around that belly. My armpits grew damp and a hot feeling rose from my stomach to my cheeks. What could I do, what could I take back? I got out of the car, walked around to the passenger-side door, and helped her out. Mostly I wanted to be rid of Gail and her hormones, her rings clink-clinking around her neck.

"It's fine, it's fine," I said, leading her to her car.

"I just can't even imagine," she shuddered. "It's so awful. I'm sorry. I'll stop in a second. It's the hormones, you know?"

I didn't know.

"Just let me ask you," Gail said. "Do you mind?"

My pulse still raced. "What?"

She caught her breath. "Was it anything you, um, anything you did?"

I stared at her, uncomprehending.

"I mean was it something you did," she said again. "Did you read the books? Because I've read all the books. I'm doing what they tell you to do. What was it? What did you do wrong?"

I had no answer for Gail. We stared at each other for a while, and I kept silent. I never think of what I want to say until later, anyway. I turned on my heel, boots crunching on the salted pavement. I was reaching for my car door handle when I heard Gail call "Wait!" She shuffled toward me, her eyes filled with wet concern. Regret, too. Here she came. Legs bowed, her balloon belly bouncing up and down. My hand clenching, my arm swinging, Gail not stopping.

Resuscitation

Shel always blushes when she gives mouth-to-mouth. She wears her wheat-brown hair pulled back so the class can monitor the movement of her cheeks, the air leaving her body for the rubbery torso of Roberto, the perma-tanned CPR dummy, something of a hunk. Shel covers her mouth with one hand when she smiles—a childhood habit to hide her teeth—but mouth-to-mouth exposes her. Years back, her younger sister Betsy got braces, but Shel had refused. Adamant about all those appointments, the rubber bands and headgear, the ache that Betsy said she still felt, a phantom pain, ten years after getting her metal removed. Shel wonders if she must look like a rabbit, moving teeth-first to fill a dummy with air. She wonders what she would look like as an adult with braces, whether she'd snag Roberto's comatose lips.

"I can't see," complains Ian, Betsy's fiancé, here in his future sister-in-law's class as part of a work requirement. Shel gets plenty of firefighters and cops and babysitters, but she never knew therapists needed CPR. Ian's practice had had An Incident.

"Turn my way?" Ian stares her down, grinning. He reminds her of a handsome cockatiel, with his spiky hair, beaky nose, and fathomless eyes. Shel is not in love with her sister's fiancé, no way. But for some reason, she does sometimes imagine cooking dinner for him, naked. It's that little look he gives her, which to her mind communicates a hunger that could be satisfied in two ways. Ew, she censors herself, then plans a menu anyway: duck confit, a pear cake, crisp potatoes fried into crunchy shoestrings. She admonishes herself in the same thought: Ian gives that look to anything in a skirt. And Shel, as a rule, wears khaki pants. But she turns to demo for Ian anyway. She wants him to see her skill, to get his money's worth.

"That's better," Ian says. "Yes. Excellent."

Nervous, Shel finishes the breaths more quickly, more forcefully, than normal. Roberto's lungs, were they real instead of synthetic, would burst from the pressure. She stands and smooths the front of her chinos. The finger sweep isn't until next class, but Shel gives a preview: you have to be prepared, she tells the group, to remove any number of everyday household items: pen caps, batteries, action figures, croutons, dice, marbles, crayons, coins. "And that's just off the top of my head," she warns her students. A pert woman who had introduced herself as a grandmother-to-be, maybe forty and wearing a clingy white tank top, shudders visibly. She mouths the word *coins*, eyes shut in reverse rapture.

L adder Company 12 is celebrating its recertification with shots at the Dalmatian. Shel throws back giant thimbles of whiskey like a civic duty: pride mixed with resignation. The firefighters supply more drinks each time. It isn't even four-thirty in the afternoon. She's agreed to be home by seven for another dress fitting with Betsy.

"You should see her with Roberto," hoots one of the crew-cut kids. "Damn!" He reaches behind the bartender's back to ring the tip bell, twice.

"It's hot," agrees another in his Brooklynese. *Hawt.* They are typical of the guys she goes out with, eager and pleasantly uncomplicated, committing to week-long relationships at best. It's nice when they stretch into two weekends.

Shel smiles demurely, covering her teeth with her lips. Then with another shot glass.

A few minutes later she is navigating the narrow stairs down to the basement to change the keg. She doesn't work at the bar, but is there often enough to know how things work. And she's been helped out by the bartender numerous times: a cab call or two, a clarifying to her beer goggling ("No, not him.") Was there anyone Fat Lloyd would approve of? His was a kindly fat, a beer fat, that made him appear much older than he really was, and he treated all customers but Shel with grim acquiescence. She didn't know how old he really was, but often felt surprise when he chimed in on a bit of '80s music trivia (Dead or Alive's single chart-topping hit, "You Spin Me Round (Like a Record)" or displayed his skill at reciting *Brady Bunch* trivia, both from the show itself, and also the tell-all memoirs that nearly all the child actors had written in midlife. His cultural touchstones marked him as around her age. Unkindly, Shel thought he was probably just a couch potato, given to overindulgence of both television and snack foods. Though she had to admit that *she* knew most of the answers, too.

The basement is dank but clean, the keg lines easy to navigate. Shel is good with her hands and excels at almost any mechanical task. The job takes less than five minutes, but she isn't ready to rejoin the party. It's quiet in the basement, calm. She turns down the hall and lingers at the open door of Fat Lloyd's office. Pennants for sports teams adorn the walls, beside framed and autographed eight-by-ten glossies of celebrities who had visited the bar (Bette Midler, Harry Connick Jr., Denzel Washington— all in town on separate movie shoots), and a picture of his father, Tall Lloyd, who ran the bar up until his death two years prior. The funeral was the same day as the *Frasier* finale, and following the services, Shel and a bunch of regulars had watched the show together at the Dalmatian. It had been Tall Lloyd's favorite after *Cheers* went off the air.

A computer whirrs atop the corner desk. Shel sits in Fat Lloyd's office chair, which is too big for her. She hasn't been down here in years. She isn't drunk, but the whiskey has wrapped around her brain like a fuzzy blanket. When she clicks on the computer screen, an internet window appears for an online dating site. YOU ARE LOGGED OFF, the page states. What Shel would give for a password. She has always loved knowing things about people that they didn't know she knew: scouring Betsy's journal for her teenage indiscretions against unwitting boyfriends, looking through her parents' bill file and discovering, despite their frugality and claims to mod- est means, astronomical stock portfolios. Her secret findings always reas- sured her. That life could be lived as understatement or exaggeration. That there were multiple versions of truth, none necessarily wrong. Or right. Look at all the space that opened up. Wiggle room.

She isn't sure DateMatch would reassure her about Fat Lloyd, or herself. Whatever truths or untruths were revealed might be too much to look at, like the sun during an eclipse. She turns the monitor off, pityingly; also, with awe. Good for Fat Lloyd. She wouldn't have the guts. It had never occurred to her. It was occurring to her now, a little, in subconscious increments.

Back upstairs, when the Brooklynese firefighter puts his arm around Shel's waist, and Shel automatically puts her hand over her mouth, Fat Lloyd shakes his head. "She's a lady, my friend," Fat Lloyd tells the kid. "Gotta know how to treat a lady."

The kid grins and removes his arm and stands before Shel to perform a sweeping bow.

"Lady," he trills theatrically. "Want another drink?"

Fat Lloyd doesn't wait for Shel's response. "Jesus Christ," he says, turning his back on them to watch the overhead TV. Sox/Cubs, Crosstown Classic. "Lemme know how this shakes out."

After a beat, he turns to Shel and winks. She knew that in a moment he would roll his eyes, because he always did, and as usual she wasn't sure if he was exasperated with himself, with her, or with the guy who wasn't living up to the standards Fat Lloyd seemed to have set for her. All these standards. Implied, clear as the globular wine glasses hanging from the rack: somebody had to set them, since she certainly hasn't.

"Watch this!" the young firefighter calls, and tilts his head back to balance a full pint of beer on his forehead. He doesn't spill a drop.

The weather is finally nice after a rainy spring, and Shel is too tipsy to drive, so she walks the fifteen blocks home. The early evening sunshine takes on the color of light shining through a whiskey bottle.

Shel's sister is coming for the dress fitting, and Shel will be late. Never mind that their parents could let Betsy in—they have the spare keys. Shel occupies one-half of a duplex owned by her parents. They live on the other side, so quiet that she had a hard time knowing when they're home. In her own second-floor bedroom window, she can see the silhouette waiting for her: the dress dummy that stands upright, a woman with a stick up her ass. Shel had learned to sew in high school theater productions, where the drama teacher pulled her from Home Ec in a frothy, key-jangling panic, demanding harem pants for fifteen extra concubines. Shel had complied, using a drapey silk that unintentionally modernized the garments with a 1990s MC Hammer sensibility. Future generations now could watch not only *The King and I* restored on DVD, but a quasi-homage to "U Can't Touch This." The seamstress's well-meaning, nimble fingers are poison to preservation. People date everything they touch. Like Shel's old wedding gown, which she had pulled over the dummy's headless form. It was no more timeless: the poufy sleeves and lace and beading of a bygone era, of *America's Funniest Home Videos*, of a mistake.

Shel wouldn't have minded if Betsy had let herself in. She would have preferred it, to save time, small talk, the necessary niceties. But Betsy wants her older sister there at the moment she lifts the dress from the dummy and pulls the silk over her head. She wants her there for everything.

"You're late," Betsy trills cheerfully, sitting on the stoop ⟨ ⟩aper cup of designer coffee in each hand. She tilts her head to sweep her ⟨ ⟩ el- highlighted bangs from her eyes.

"I can't have caffeine at this hour," Shel says.

"Got you decaf, dummy," Betsy says. "But which is which? Hmm."

She smiles with those straight teeth. Smiles with all her might, which is considerable. "I could taste-test it," she says. "But I shouldn't have too much coffee, what with the teeth-whitening and all . . ." She carefully inserts a straw through one lid.

The wedding is in two weeks. Betsy and Ian shall be bonded forever, in all their bonded and capped and bleached grinning glory, following a cer- emony with a Catholic Mass. The last six months have been filled with stipulations, appointments, excuses. Betsy couldn't help plant the family vegetable garden because she might get bug bites or poison ivy. Or bad tan lines. No, dinner would not work that night, or most other nights; she had Pilates followed by a deep breathing mat workout. No dessert for her, even if it was her birthday and Shel had made a German chocolate cake, both Betsy and Ian's favorite. There was the dress to keep in mind.

The dress. Shel's dress.

Shel had made it herself. She had worn it many times, but never to her own wedding. The family, as was their way, didn't talk about it. Not in the months leading up to the canceled date, not in the years after, not when Rob, her intended, moved two towns over and married someone else (she had heard they divorced in less than a year, which did not surprise her). And they espe- cially did not talk about the time Shel had come downstairs from her side of the duplex in the gorgeous handmade gown on what was supposed to be her wedding day, and walked to the corner for a six pack and some magazines. She carried her money in the small white beaded clutch she had found a year before at the Bridal Emporium on the boulevard. Then she walked home, climbed the steps, and stayed inside for a week. Leave me alone, she had said, and they did. The neighbor kids rang the bell and ran, swearing they had seen a woman in a wedding dress standing in the window on a Wednesday after- noon, plain as the silk taffeta draping her somewhat concave bodice. She never answered the door. Maybe these were just stories, taking shape in the town's chatter, the way people make things up to understand whatever it is they don't understand. You could blame the gossips. But maybe they simply were trying to get history down intact. Floating false information to flush out the truth.

Betsy was the only one to broach the subject. And one could easily argue her interest was not for Shel's well-being: she left the issue alone for approximately seven years. It seemed pertinent, relevant, for her to finally ask about Shel and her handmade dress, because she wondered if it would be all right to wear it for her own wedding. Betsy showed remarkable restraint, for her part: she waited about an hour after Ian's proposal. She did not say "wedding" or "gown" or "bride." She asked Shel, without really asking, "Maybe I'd wear the dress you sewed."

"Why not," Shel had said, setting down her milk glass at the hastily arranged family dinner. Their parents looked from one daughter to the next, then studied the pot roast on their plates. Ian was with a thousand other therapists in Telluride at an anger management conference. He had proposed by webcam.

"Super!" Betsy cried. "I haven't got an inch on my credit cards, but that's not why I want to wear it. I always loved that dress. Think you can help me alter it?"

Shel shrugged her indifference and asked to be passed the potatoes. Everybody knew Betsy was hopeless with a needle and thread. "Helping" meant Shel would do all the work. Shel mentally steeled herself for the task. It would bring some settled muck back to the surface. Everyone assumed she had been left by Rob. Some even told a story that involved Shel standing forlornly at the altar, petals falling from her bouquet, but it had never gone that far. When the wedding was called off two months before the date, Shel had been the one to cancel the vendors, to arrange for partial refunds, to take care of all the details, and she hadn't minded that much. Not like you might expect of an ex-bride-to-be. Instead she was filled with a kind of relief and gratitude that she wouldn't spend her life married to Rob. The two of them, oddly still loyal, vowed not to tell anyone why the wedding wouldn't go on as planned, which meant people would draw their own conclusions. People always do, anyway, even when the facts are laid out before them like playing cards.

But the dress. The dress had been special. She had been looking forward to wearing that dress. Shel designed it herself, spending weeks sketching in her big art pad, making erasures, sketching again. The fabric sifted through her hands not like water, but something softer, thicker, like cream if cream took fabric form. She created an underlay that wouldn't itch the sensitive skin of her legs, or her other under-areas. People don't know how tulle can scratch.

Still, Betsy wants tulle. "This dress is gorgeous in its simplicity," she says now, twirling before the mirror. "But the style today calls for, like, a little oomph. I need a little oomph under my dress!"

She laughs and crouches in a pose, Marilyn Monroe-over-the-steam-grate, but to Shel the laugh sounds fake. Betsy has already laid claim: *my dress.*

"That's still going to be mine," Shel says evenly through the pins in her mouth. "I'm letting you wear the dress."

"Oh," Betsy says. "Oh. Well. You can always take the poufy stuff out, right?"

"The tulle I don't mind," Shel says. In fact, a new bolt bought just for this purpose sits inside the hall closet. "Just call things what they are, OK?"

Betsy ignores this. Next door, there's the sound of a chair scraping heavily across the floor—their father's gesture, one which drove their mother crazy—then silence. In the way of their family, Betsy changes the subject. "Ian says you're a really good teacher. He says he can see why the YMCA put you in charge of the first aid program."

Ian is one class away from his own graduation. Shel can't help it: she'll miss having him in class. Of course she'll be seeing a lot of him with the upcoming wedding festivities. But that's not really the same thing. She has no special skills at weddings, nothing of note that might attract attention or set her apart from the rest of the guests, aside from creating a dress she won't be wearing. As the unmarried sister of the bride, it might be nice, she thought, to find a date. Briefly the dating website enters her mind, but only briefly. What if Fat Lloyd saw her? Or one of the other guys she had gone home with from the bar. There had been more than a few. What if any of them turned out to be one of her matches?

Betsy interrupts these imaginings. "Shel? Can we talk about these big sleeves? Since we're updating the style and all. It's just that I've always pictured myself in a sleeveless dress."

Shel stifles her sigh with a sip of coffee. Caffeinated. Her heart races, and still she swallows more than she should.

In class the next day, Shel corrects a preteen girl on her form with chest compressions, and tears spring to the girl's eyes. Shel knows she has not been particularly harsh: this is merely the way of some girls, even responsible ones who want to learn how to be Safe Sitters, a designation bestowed on those who complete a course that certifies they know how not to kill the babies with which they've been entrusted. Still, Shel feels a twinge of remorse. Later she is sure to complement the girl, who sports a midriff T-shirt that says BRAT, on a successful finger sweep of Roberto the CPR dummy's fishlike mouth. When she pats BRAT on the back, Ian gives Shel a complicit grin. She grins back, forgetting to cover her mouth; her teeth are not as bad as she thinks, anyway. Shel pictures making Ian a dinner of bright raw fruits and sautéed vegetables, wearing only an apron and high heels, which, as a rule, she abhors. The heels would be red, to match the strawberries and red peppers. They would eat off of pristine white ceramic, those heavy plates sold at restaurant supply shops. Then they would smash the dirty plates on the floor. She doesn't get much further than the plate-smashing. That might be enough.

Shel isn't optimistic about Betsy and Ian's future. This could be due to her generally pessimistic nature surrounding weddings. Or it's the accumulation of her observations. Ian owned a pair of binoculars and claimed to be an avid bird watcher, but he couldn't tell the difference between male and female cardinals. Even Shel, who paid nature only brief perfunctory glances, knew that red cardinals were boys. In nature, the male birds get all the showy plumage. And Betsy's always been flighty. She never held onto her money or held down any job aside from office temp work. She had been the fill-in receptionist at Ian's practice two years ago, where they met. Maybe Betsy's grown out of her cheating phase, but Shel watches her sister when Ian's talking, and Betsy's mind is usually somewhere else. The tiniest smile will play across her mouth when Ian's describing how therapists can get secondary trauma from listening to patients' stories. "I mean," he would say at a family dinner, "things so awful you wouldn't expect them in a horror film. Housewares used as instruments of torture." Ian's face would cloud over like a little boy's, and Shel felt for him, she really did. Betsy would be stirring her minestrone with her spoon, a lazy, luxurious movement, with a half smile on her face. She was in the habit of checking her teeth in the reflection offered by the back of the spoon. All clear. Shel thought their marriage would be a different kind of torture, with household items as props. Phone bills listing unfamiliar numbers. A pair of binoculars and a neighbor who failed to pull her shades. A soup spoon reflecting only one person, but a distorted reflection, features out of proportion.

Fat Lloyd had known Shel's ex-fiancé, who had come into the bar several nights a week. This was when Rob was working at the travel agency down the street, and he would bring home stacks of obsolete brochures and oblong folders to use as scrap paper. Shel might receive a phone message scrawled on the back of a Gettysburg battlefield reenactment scene. Rob wrote so the words looked like they were coming from the old-fashioned cannon: CALL YOUR MOTHER. He had excellent handwriting.

One night, Shel had gotten to the Dalmatian before Rob. Business was slow and Fat Lloyd was belly-up to the bar, watching an old episode of *The Honeymooners*. "Pull up a seat," he had said.

They watched together in silence until the commercial break, then Fat Lloyd got her a beer. He popped the bottle cap and said, "Heard you're making quite the dress."

Shel covered her mouth and smiled. She was proud of her work, proud that Rob had taken an interest. He helped her without even asking, nearly every night. Then Fat Lloyd surprised her by describing, almost bead-by-bead, what her wedding gown looked like. The train that could be bustled. The princess sleeves. And, Lloyd said pointedly, the material that felt better than anything he had ever felt.

"He?" Shel asked. "You mean Rob?"

Fat Lloyd looked at her with a good deal of kindness, with some sadness mixed in. "Yeah, him," he said.

"Well, he better like it," she said defensively, not wanting to hear what the bartender was implying. "With all the work I'm putting in. I'm lucky he cares so much."

"About you, though?" Fat Lloyd asked. He rearranged pint glasses, mercifully not looking at her.

"Who else?" she laughed, and then her stomach turned into a stone.

Lloyd did look at her then. He spoke quietly. No way could any of the other customers hear him. "So he likes dresses," he said. "Who am I to argue? I like stupid old TV shows." He grabbed the bottle cap from her beer off the bar, holding it between thumb and forefinger. Without looking, he flicked it behind his back and into the trash can.

"It's not that, Shel," he said. "He brings in guys he says are clients. I've been here a long time. I know some of 'em. I'm sorry, honey, but they aren't booking flights."

Right then, Shel felt that she should indicate her surprise in some way. She was aware of the need to show that open-mouthed expression, along with her shock and betrayal: all appropriate emotions. But she experienced none of those things. There had been a feeling nagging at her for as long as she'd labored over the dress. Longer. She appreciated Rob's interest. No one in her family had cared about helping with a hem or straightening a crooked seam, but Rob would bring her pincushion and thread and sit nearby, asking questions. The two of them had scoffed at the superstition about seeing the dress before the wedding. She had been pleased to be with a man who wasn't a cliché.

She'd felt only the briefest wave of dread, easily swallowed and choked down, the day she had come home from teaching class and seen Rob standing before the tall mirror in their bedroom, holding her wedding dress up against the length of his naked body. He had been startled, then quickly calmed, calming her. People get curious, she reasoned then. And Rob had told her he was getting a sense of the alterations left to be done. Since they were the same height. More off the bottom, didn't she think?

What made her angrier than anything else was that he had turned out to be a cliché after all. Then she was sad. Followed by angry. Mixed with some more sad. And pity, an emotion she would learn to detest deflecting, the main reason she stayed inside her duplex for a week, wearing her wedding dress at will. But at the time, in that moment at the bar with Fat Lloyd, she had yet to know the uselessness of pity: she quickly transitioned to pitying Rob, who felt unable to be who he was. Poor Rob!

When Rob arrived at the bar that night, Fat Lloyd offered them the use of his office. Twenty businesslike minutes later, they had sorted their stories and how to handle the details. Rob asked for discretion, which she was happy to provide. Shel's silence, keeping him in the closet along with her wedding dress, made people wonder. What kind of woman wouldn't show grief at a canceled wedding? What kind of woman would let a guy like Rob Hatch get away? It was all on her. To her knowledge, nobody speculated about Rob. To them he would always be the same charming guy who sang the national anthem at the Founders' Day parade, who gave them insider information on Mediterranean cruises, who humorously mangled the words to "American Pie" at karaoke night. And he still was that guy. Lucky for Shel, she had learned another way to see him before things had gone too far.

Shel had little regret about how things turned out. She could look back and see all the ways she had been warned—phone hang-ups late at night, broken lunch dates, a distance in his eyes when they kissed. If other people had seen Rob's dates at the Dalmatian and been suspicious, they didn't say. Only Fat Lloyd had been observant enough, kind enough, to see what was going on and tell her. Fat Lloyd who kept to himself and stayed out of it, except when it came to Shel. And she had trusted him so completely, so immediately, that she ended her engagement in the bar's basement office without hesitation. She hadn't even cried. And the bartender had been right: Rob immediately agreed with everything she said. No, it was all for the best. Shel had cared little about a big wedding, or being a bride, or any of the trappings Betsy now obsessed over: matching chair covers at the reception, for God's sake.

If she did have a regret, it was the dress. What had possessed her to keep it, allowing for it now to be given away? Why had she not cut it into ribbons and tossed them into the wind, giving birds materials for their nests? She had stowed it in the closet like some average garment. She had loved, still loved, the dress. It was hers and always would be. Even when Betsy put it on, tulle added, sleeves removed, and marched the altered version to the altar.

Ian's CPR/First Aid course ends on a Friday afternoon, and the legal-age members of the class head down the block to the Dalmatian. The wedding is in one week and one day, and Betsy pulls herself away early from that day's spa treatments to join them. A posse of giggling bridesmaids are summoned. Shel, maid of honor, is the alleged head of this group, but these pushy girls took over any and all arrangements, and all parties were pleased with the arrangement. They mime how they will jockey for the bride's bouquet. They draw on cocktail napkins the order in which they will traipse down the aisle on the arms of Ian's brothers and golf buddies. Before long, the event takes on the festive air of a rehearsal dinner. There are toasts, manicure comparisons, complexion reassurances, last-minute orders regarding who will bring what item to the church, though it is far from the last minute. The last minute, Shel thinks, is before you say those words you can't easily take back: "I do." But of course people take them back all the time, sparing no difficulty. Even last minutes can stretch across eons. Even last minutes can be undone.

The happy couple is busy talking to other people. Ian works the room, becoming blurry with perpetual motion. Betsy stands at the center of her bridal court. She is tan and firm of bicep. Her sundress dangles strappily off delicate shoulders, her diamond necklace sparkles in the hollow of her collarbone.

"Jesus, Betsy, could you look any hotter?" says Angelica, the chief organizing bridesmaid, who sports fire engine red fingernails and snaps picture after digital picture. "You are going to be such a hot bride, girl. Everyone in this room is jealous of you right now."

If Fat Lloyd hears all this, Shel can't tell. He's in work mode and brings Shel whatever she asks for, and a couple things she doesn't. "On the house," he says. "It's graduation day."

In the pre-wedding commotion, she's nearly forgotten her CPR charges, who have been pushed to the periphery: a daycare owner, one rookie firefighter from Ladder Company 12, the fortyish soon-to-be grandmother who admits her fear that she will be stuck raising her reckless teenage daughter's baby. Shel sends them a round of drinks, including one for Ian.

When Fat Lloyd pulls the tap for the Bud Light, it sputters foam. Shel jumps up. "I'll get it," she says, and heads downstairs to change the keg. The other bartender, Phil, nods his thanks. Happy Hour is the Dalmatian's busiest time of the week.

It's a relief to be in the cool basement, to be alone. Like last time, she finishes the task quickly and eases into Fat Lloyd's office chair. The computer is turned off. She leans her head back and closes her eyes, trying to distinguish the various voices above her head, the stabbing of stilettos into the wood-plank floor, the shuffling clump of men's thick-soled dress shoes.

"Comfy?"

Shel's eyes snap open like window shades. Fat Lloyd is smirking at her. She starts to get up, but he motions for her to stay put. He settles into a creaky wooden chair on the other side of the old wooden desk, as if she were interviewing him for a job.

"You holding up OK?" he asks. Rather than answer, Shel picks up the Magic 8 Ball resting next to the keyboard. She gives it a shake, then holds it out for him to see: BETTER NOT TELL YOU NOW. They smile at one another with their mouths, not their eyes.

"Ian's a shitty tipper," Fat Lloyd confides, his hands clasped over his big belly.

"Actually, I think I forgot to tip after the last round," Shel remembers.

"You get dispensation," he says.

"What for?"

He rolls his eyes comically to the ceiling, where patrons creak the floorboards from the other side. "You're bar family," he says. "We're supposed to take each other for granted."

The footsteps on the stairs are Ian's; he knocks on the doorframe and steps inside. "Betsy's looking for you, Shel," he says. "It's about her wedding dress—she's lost more weight or something."

"Be right up," Shel says, though Ian's already clomping up the stairs. She is no longer thinking of naked dinners. Fat Lloyd gathers some papers off the desk and shuffles them around in his hands, acting like a bartender who's busy doing something other than eavesdropping.

"It's my dress," she tells him softly.

He drops the sheaf of papers. "She's wearing your dress?" Fat Lloyd's eyebrows shoot up. "*The* dress? No. She doesn't deserve it."

Shel is conflicted. On the one hand, she agrees with Lloyd, her benevolent protector, her bar family, the big brother she never had. On the other hand, Betsy is her real family. Her baby sister in braces, always in braces, even with straight teeth, even as a hot bride. Betsy was just a kid who knew what she wanted and went for it. There was something to be said for that.

"There's something to be said for . . ." Shel starts, but can't finish.

Lloyd watches her face carefully, and she doesn't look away. She studies him back. Extra weight ages people, even children. They get treated older than they are, taken for small, middle-aged adults. She knows from pictures that Fat Lloyd's been big all his life. She remembers his silent father behind the bar, smirking when patrons differentiated between him and his son. Shel looks at Lloyd now as if seeing him for the first time. His eyes are young. His gaze unsettles her.

On the desk are the paper printouts—his matches from the dating site. He sees her looking but doesn't cover up the pages. His profile picture shows him pulling the Guinness tap. The lighting's a little dark, but it's a good likeness. Women will know who they're getting with this one.

She's about to ask how the dating is going when he blurts, "I saw you in your dress."

"My wedding dress?"

"I came by that day to see if you wanted company. I was parked down the street, trying to decide if I should ring the bell. I didn't know if you wanted to be alone, or what. And I felt sorta responsible. About the wedding not happening and all."

"You saw me in my dress?" Shel has a single focus now. She fails to hear what else he is telling her.

"Oh, yeah," he says. "Yeah. Walking down the block like you owned it. You looked nice. Very pretty. You know."

She does know, though nobody had ever told her. She had made that dress for herself, and she wore it well on the day she was supposed to. And after all this time: somebody had seen. And not just neighborhood kids who thought she was strange and hilarious, somebody who didn't matter. She had been seen for who she was, for who she wanted to be. Not a bride, necessarily. Only this: a person who made a beautiful thing and was worthy of it.

"Hey, thank you," she says. "I mean it. Let's go back to the party, okay?"

He pauses as if he's going to say something, then shakes his head. "C'mon, kiddo," is all he says.

She senses his deflation, unable to pinpoint herself as its cause. She walks ahead of him on the stairs, conscious of his labor up the short flight. Instinctively she slows, turning to ask if he's okay. The trainer in her is mentally practicing chest compressions, calculating the pressure she would have to apply for a man his size, wondering how she to get his body to the landing if needed. Performing CPR on the stairs wouldn't be ideal, but she could manage.

Fat Lloyd rests one hand on his heart. His color's good, though his eyes are a bit flatter than they were back in the office. Shel wants to take his pulse. He waves her off.

"I'm good," he assures her. "Though I could always be better."

They blink their way into the still-daylight of the bar like a couple of moles. Ian and Betsy are in the middle of a passionate discussion. Over what, appetizer choices? Whose teeth are whitest? Ian disengages first, framing Shel and Fat Lloyd with his hands as if to take a picture. Somebody's Nikon sits on the bar, but nobody makes a move for it.

"On three," Ian calls, preparing to click the pretend shutter.

Shel moves a little closer to Fat Lloyd. He is catching his breath and puts his shaky hand at the small of her back. Shel leans against Lloyd and the two of them freeze, smiling on cue, acting as if this counts.

I'm Not Who You Think I Am

The fact of the matter is, the man I am scheduled to marry in one month has disappeared and taken his inheritance with him. I'm not the kind of girl who would say money changes everything, because I don't believe it's true. I want to believe we're better than that. But it changed some things. Him, for one. Me, for another.

Derry came into the money at the perfect time: six months before our wedding. Some people might shrug at an inheritance of fifty thousand dollars—a year's salary, a nest egg, something to sock away for a rainy day or midlife splurge. Money to plant and grow in some sort of investment incubator. For us, it meant the wedding would be covered, and then some.

Derry had other ideas. And wouldn't I like to know what they are. Wouldn't I like to know where to find him, so I could ask.

Being out of touch wasn't so unusual, so I waited two days after Derry disappeared before calling family and friends. I thought I needed to file a missing persons report. At the police station, I scanned the cars in the parking lot, foolishly searching for his Chevrolet Caprice, even though I had been there when it was repossessed in the middle of the night by a brisk little woman with straw-blond hair and a gun. A misunderstanding, Derry said, though that was weeks ago and still no car. He borrowed a van from one of the guys who played drums in his band. Items from our house disappeared more gradually, less dramatically, so that when Derry, too, vanished, I could not pin down for the police how long the closed stereo cabinet had been missing its components. The china vase: when had I last seen it? I had kept my grandfather's World War II compass wrapped in a handkerchief in my underwear drawer; that was gone, too. An investigator came to the house and took notes. He was tall, with a nose that looked like it had been broken at least twice. "An inside job," the detective said, while I nodded and stared at the worn linoleum. I thought about Derry's side of the closet, which was half-empty as usual, like he was only visiting. Not all of the things missing were mine, I rationalized. Some were his to lose.

His sister was unconcerned when I called with the news that Derry was missing.

"Cold feet," said Sherryl over the phone. "Lord knows you're not the first woman he's walked out on." My sister-in-law-to-be sighed like a steamboat at my questions. No, she knew nothing of her brother's whereabouts. Or that of my missing vase and stereo and red leather coat. "Did you check any of the pawn shops? That might be a good starting point."

I started crying. She relented, sort of.

"He pulls this shit all the time," she said. "It won't be long before he pops up out of his little rabbit hole."

But he hadn't. Derry missed a gig he was supposed to play with the band. They were more like a dis-band, with a rotating membership depending on who was or wasn't strung out on speed or back in County for thirty days on "trumped up bullshit charges." Those who subbed in earned petty cash until the shady prodigals returned. It was Derry's turn to fill in for the guitarist, who had an honest job as a contractor and was helping build a house a few hours north, in the middle of the Michigan woods. Sometimes Greg hired Derry to do construction work around town—small carpentry and drywall jobs—but he wasn't in Michigan. Greg was pissed to hear that Derry had missed the gig, so I knew he wasn't just covering for him. Derry's real job was picking up shifts driving a truck throughout the Midwest; he was on a sub list, no benefits. I called dispatch. They hadn't heard a peep.

That's what worries me. The Derry I know is so loud, he couldn't hide if he tried.

For days I paced the house like a nervous cat, avoiding work. The second-floor window gave a view of the far acres, where progress on a new subdivision had stalled. A backhoe sat alone on the edge of the empty field. Ages ago they had brought in bulldozers and cleared the land, stripped it to the brown dirt, which had grown a new expanse of weeds that almost looked like a lawn from a distance. Then they took all the equipment away. Only that little backhoe remained, tiny as a toy in the distance.

Derry practically lived here. It's a small, cramped Cape Cod rented in my name, the land out back a deal-closer. We would go out on warm nights and throw stones into the field, comparing how far we could pitch. Sometimes we took a bottle of whiskey, a couple beers, and we would throw until our arms hung limp. We talked ourselves hoarse, though there were times we didn't say a thing. When Uncle Roy, the last of Derry's distant, elderly relatives, kicked the bucket, he sent fifty thousand dollars each to Derry and Sherryl. Derry suggested putting the money down on a new house. One we could build, one that would be ours instead of mine, even though this was just a place I had rented. Derry had gotten ahold of blueprints for one of the models in the new subdivision and spread them across the dining room table. I murmured that it would be nice, but of course we had the cost of the wedding to consider. He nodded, rolling up his plans, which I never saw again.

I needed a distraction. I finally turned on the computer and logged in. Work sent me the latest cases, which I downloaded and perused over coffee. Years ago I signed a confidentiality agreement that I was not supposed to discuss details of my occupation with anyone, and a waiver that stated I was ethically bound to turn down any case in which I held "significant emotional attachment." But when I opened the file with Sherryl's name on it, there was no deliberating. I had to act fast before another agent grabbed the offer.

ACCEPT? the computer asked me, and I clicked the button marked YES! Jazzy animation filled the screen, a dancing sleuth in a trench coat with arms clasped in victory, professional sporting event muzak ("Let's get ready to rumble!"), the works. My company's tagline scrolled across the screen: TRACK 'EM DOWN!

Client name: Sherryl Chance
Object/Pursuant: Derrick "Derry" Chance
Reason for initializing case (child support, alimony, back taxes, etc.): Because he is my brother who I love dearly. (Also he owes me $$.)
Other family and locations: None. Six feet under. The little shit is all I have left.
Appearance (please include a photo): Handsome! In the spirit of Clark Gable, mixed with David Blaine (FYI, that magician who chains himself to things and doesn't eat, though I believe he is half-black, and Derry is all white. More the style of David Blaine: cool guy with leather jacket. Scruffy/hot. Not that I think my brother is hot.) He has a port-color shamrock-shaped birthmark on his left butt cheek. Tattoo of girl's name on right shoulder.

47

(Of course she means *my* name. She couldn't bring herself to write it. I scribbled it on the printout. The picture is one I recognize from a Fourth of July barbecue last summer: she's cut me out, though you can see part of my tanned arm. Derry looks drunk and haphazard, and exactly as she described him.)

Will object flee if confronted, or act in a volatile manner? YES. Derry always does what he wants and doesn't know what's good for him. I miss my dumbass little brother so much! You should know he owes me $50,000, my half of our inheritance, which I loaned him for a new investment. He wouldn't tell me what it was. I trusted him.

I trusted him, too. Derry was the only one who knew my real job. I worked at home, with databases and computer searches, which I had already used—unsuccessfully—to hunt for Derry. Usually, it was easier than you would think. People who allegedly didn't want to be found left behind a trail of clues. Guilt breadcrumbs. We located the missing in any number of relatively simple ways. Through smartphone use. What they liked on Facebook. An undeleted internet browser history, or one they thought they had deleted. A credit card statement that correlated a gas stop with a nearby hotel bill.

What a bunch of careless slobs, with their philandering and drinking and unpaid bar bets, their small betrayals that sent them running. Derry, then, was far more crafty, far more careful. I had tried the usual channels and met nothing but dead ends. With any other case, I would close it, offer condolences, and collect payment. But this was Derry. He would know to use cash, to disguise himself, to travel in ways that left no record or trace. After all, he had learned those tricks from me.

My front was a secret shopper, paid to browse the mall and eat appetizers and guzzle martinis, and to undergo an occasional outpatient cosmetic procedure, so long as the effects were not permanent. It's how I would sometimes go undercover: a collagen injection here, a color rinse there, and bam, you might think you know me, but then you're not sure. Derry would startle at my plumped lips, my dramatically arched eyebrows. He recovered quickly. "When are they going to give you the big cazongas?" he would ask, making man's universal, two-handed gesture for big boobs.

"I don't see you complaining," I said, unbuttoning my shirt.

"Darlin,'" Derry grinned wickedly, reaching for me, "if I had a reason to complain, I'd be gone. And I am decidedly here."

Until he wasn't.

My screen dinged: CONFIRMED. GO GET 'EM!

I drove to the grocery story, my mind whirring with new data. Sherryl had provided several new leads in the file she unwittingly dropped in my lap. Derry liked strip clubs in neighboring towns. His favorite fast food, Rax, was hours and states away. I mentally calculated the cost of a road trip, how many jobs I would need to take. I tried to imagine his reaction at being found; the best I could picture was resignation. He had left. Was I really supposed to give chase, desperate and vengeful? Historically, Derry preferred to do the chasing. But I wanted answers. Only he could give them.

I shopped and worked a job simultaneously: feedback on the new organic grocery. My eyes swam through the different shades of lettuce, the colorful packages of dried fruits and nuts. I settled on granola bars for the road. Honestly, carob cookies are my mother's thing, not mine. My appetite is nil. Grief—or whatever this is—has turned my body thin, and damned if Derry isn't here to see it. He's everywhere and nowhere: I've found traces of Derry in the bag boys, the single men shopping in slacks and ties and pre-distressed leather coats (as if to say, "I work! But I can also cut loose."), guys who were nothing like Derry, but might turn their heads a certain way, or set their shoulders just so: Derry getting defensive, Derry preparing a monologue about The Problem with You, who would be me.

I thought we had resolved our last fight. Derry always insisted that if something was wrong, we had to say it: whatever choked us off from each other, or from ourselves, or lived between us like a pet or a docile child, something to protect, or to keep us from killing one another. Just say it, he would tell me, all the times I was struggling to speak up. The other week, during an argument about sixty bucks missing from my wallet, he goaded me into calling him white trash. Just say it, he had seethed at my silence, and I did.

"Denise, hey!" said a nervous-looking guy in a jean jacket over khakis, coaxing wet Bibb lettuce into stubborn plastic bags. "Didn't expect to see you here."

"Wrong lady," I said, still scanning the greens. Denise again. And again, and again.

This happens at least once a week. Denise, regularly, along with other names and affectionate greetings, followed by a muttered apology. People have told me I look like one of several movie actresses, dark hair and navy-blue eyes—plainly practical sidekicks. Derry and I used to joke that my type is the gal who gets the job done, cleans up the messes made by the principal players, and promptly is forgotten in the service of plot resolution. People always think they know me from somewhere.

Sometimes I'll use a standard line: I'm not who you think I am. But really I'm amazed: How can you not know your people? How can I be so generic, so expendable, like iceberg lettuce? Somehow I intuit that my doppelgangers are not striking or interesting or people worth knowing. Maybe it is because these strangers aren't thrilled to see me, whoever they think I am. Maybe it is because Derry laughed and christened me a sidekick.

The worst case of mistaken identity? I would rather not go into the details. The annals are chock-full of these moments. But once, in the type of situation you would expect (sex), under equally expected circumstances (drunk), Derry called me Denise.

Through my wine haze, I had calmly asked him, Who? He rubbed his eyes and mumbled that he'd been thinking about a certain actress. Strictly action/adventure. She was in that film, you know the one, where aliens invade Manhattan? Her character was named Denise. Reminds me of you, baby.

I never could find what movie he was talking about.

The lettuce flung droplets on my arm as the man wrestled the head into the bag. "You sure you're not Denise?" he asked. He tilted his head like a Labrador, the tilt-angle increasing when he saw my expression.

Perhaps I should've said, No, I'm not sure who I am. I didn't bother. Down the aisle, a man as tall as the top-shelf rye turned the corner, eyes last. A navy work jacket, his black hair a mess, another version of Derry. Another guy who would mistake me for someone else. But this one watched me—as if he recognized me—in a way the other ghosts had not.

My mother says it's a pickup line, a way for potential friends or lovers to approach me, because while I certainly may be a pretty girl (her words), my vibe tells people to back off.

"It's your body language," she drawled on the phone. "Nobody should be that crossed unless they're in a yoga class."

She suggested that I burn some incense, slip into an aromatic bath, cleanse my aura. I'm amazed that she didn't name me Palm Frond or Sunshine Ray or Flower.

"Maybe a little pot would help," she suggested.

"Won't that cloud my aura?" On the phone, she can't see my rolling eyes. Some spectral force probably informed her. Pot smoke reminds me of patchouli, the household perfume of my rootless, dadless childhood, a scent that makes me want to vomit.

"How did I raise such an uptight child?" One of her refrains. Easier to talk about my uptightness than the reasons for it.

"My guess is you were being practical, Ma," I said. "You needed somebody to take care of you."

"You brat," she murmured, not meanly. "Watch your karma, pumpkin face. Payback's a bitch." She asked me how I was holding up. She reminded me that I was better off alone. I hung up on her.

My free-love single mother disapproved of our engagement. When I proposed last summer, she was aghast. I expected her to be proud of my progressiveness, but she often turned traditional and paternalistic at inconvenient moments. It is true that Derry isn't—wasn't—the marrying kind. He didn't see the point. And though I had never seen myself in a poofy white dress, never dreamed of playing princess, I knew that the point of marrying Derry was Derry himself. We want to cage the cagey. I wanted to. If our wedding was turning into something grander than we actually were—the tiered chocolate raspberry ganache cake cost eight hundred dollars, and the art museum charged five grand to reserve the space—then fine. I wanted our wedding to be bigger than the both of us. It was going to be our start. It still could be.

Those stones we sailed across the field? Many were scratched with our initials, our fingernails sore, like a couple of teenagers. Sometimes I miss Derry so much my ribs ache: the thought of him tracing a finger along my jaw, or kissing me in the bar after I beat him at pool, or telling me he had never met anyone like me before, I turned him inside out, that for the rest of our lives we would be tangled together like vines.

Other times, I watched his band play, his eyes locked on a college girl pressed against the stage, a young thing with every night of the week there for the wasting. I would wait for him to look up during any number of Def Leppard covers, to see me at a barstool at the back of the room. I made it into a game: if he made eye contact before the chorus, we'd leave together after the set. Forget last call, his bandmates, all those giggling girls who wanted practice making mistakes.

The chorus, inevitably, came and went. I would swivel to face myself in the wavy mirror behind the bar, occasionally watching the distorted reflection of the band. The stage lights, I had to remind myself, were particularly blinding.

Our problems weren't that bad. Marriage was going to cement our relationship, fill in the cracks, bond us. I know now: that was foolish of me. Just because you can walk all over people doesn't mean they're the same as sidewalks.

The phone rang again and I expected my mother, ready to chastise me for hanging up on her. But it was Sherryl this time, slurring half her words. By the sound of her, she had been drinking for hours.

"The thing is," she began. Like Derry, she issued proclamations prior to actually saying anything. "The thing is, I know your game, girlfriend. Want to know how I know you so well?"

"I guess," I said.

She laughed or cried, I wasn't sure which. "Because Derry told me all about you. I know you were supposed to be some big shot at the college. Always looking down on him and me. You aren't like us. You don't need his money, so why don't you give it back to the family?"

"I don't have his money, Sherryl. Not even the deposit on our wedding cake."

"You better not be lying," she said. "I can pull your credit rating."

"Yeah, you do that," I said, distractedly piling my dirty dishes in the sink. "Bye."

I hung up. Sherryl worked for a car dealership, in collections. Her comment about college: semi-accurate. I haven't been back in years. At one point I was going for my PhD in history, a half-hearted effort, and the nightly gatherings among grad students seemed like stress relief. I didn't see them for what they were: a swinging gate missing its latch, an emergency exit. Soon I had wandered to parties on decrepit streets, my eyes substantively glazed. I approached strange porches, shy at first, then not. Edged myself to the end of town with all landmarks unknown. That was where I met Derry.

I can picture him now, on a stranger's porch at a party where we discovered that we knew only the hosts, who were huffing from aerosol cans in the garage. Getting high, DIY. Derry's face glowed in the orange burn of a cigarette. His hands moved articulately. He was summarizing a book he had read about the end of the world. It wasn't clear if the book was science or fiction or science fiction.

"Basically, the dinosaurs will come back," he said. "We'll go in reverse to this proto-world, but we won't be around to see what happens."

"You really believe that?" I asked. This guy. Who was this guy?

Derry turned to me. Someone offered him a turpentine-soaked rag, and he raised his hand, somewhat regally, to refuse. His hard face softened as he watched me, and I knew, there in a series of seconds, that we were bound for something big. Something unnameable and beautiful and disastrous. I heard a crackle inside my brain and feared he could see it in my eyes. He ran his hand through his hair, examined his hand, and then offered it to me. His palm was cool and dry.

"Speculation," he said. "We all get off on imagining our inevitable demise."

"Big words, fancy boy," a man shouted from the dark of the scabby yard. The sound of piss smacking dirt.

Derry smiled at me. "How do you think it'll end?" he asked.

I paused. How could I know the future? Derry gone, while I moved in reverse as if to start over, start new? My past felt as hazy as the life in front of me.

"Endings are overrated," I told him. I smiled hugely, showing my teeth, a frightening gesture if you think about it. But he wasn't scared. He got my meaning then, and for the next some-odd years. Until he disappeared. Wherever he is, maybe he still gets it. Maybe I still don't.

I leave the dirty dishes in the sink, crawl into bed without brushing my teeth, and turn out the lights. In the dark I make theories. Derry is hiding in a Kentucky cave, emerging long enough to stock up on Rax chicken sandwiches; he is lying in the bottom of a retention pond, trapped inside a stolen car, fish swimming through empty eye sockets; he is mangy and bereft on a Bogotá street corner, cupping change; he is eating salmon off bone china in a revolving restaurant; he is changing his identity to live a protected new life; he is fucking Denise; he is fucking Denise; he is fucking Denise. Fucking Denise.

The next afternoon, I drove fifty miles east to the Classy Chassis, a gentleman's club with a signboard that read: MEET JASMINE AND BRITTANI AND DESTYNY. PRIME RIB BUFFET $8.99. I had eaten two organic choco-granola bars in the car and declined the hostess's offer of a menu.

"Auditions aren't till tomorrow," she said, sizing me up.

I shook my head. In my best PI move, I flashed my wallet-sized photo of Derry.

"Know this guy?" I asked.

She was wearing a furry bikini and her pale white skin had reddened along the straps, as if allergic to fake fur dander. She narrowed her eyes. "Maybe. Why?"

"I'm . . . his family. He's missing, and we need any leads we can get."

"Missing? Like, what does that mean? Run off? Kidnapped? Left for dead?"

"Jesus," I said. "He's my fiancé." I teared up then. She pretended not to notice, though whatever was on my face registered with her.

"You want Destyny," she said, pointing to the stage where two women were dancing for exactly one other customer. She added helpfully, "She's the one with her top off."

I picked a table and waited for Rihanna's "SOS" to end, the tra-la-las trailing off, then laid down a five and caught Destyny's eye. She hopped off stage and pranced over. I tried not to gawk at her orange three-inch heels or her matching bikini bottom or her bare breasts. There was nowhere to look but her impeccably made-up face. I showed Derry's picture, and repeated what I had told the hostess, who watched us. They communicated via a system of nods.

"A real gentleman," Destyny said earnestly, as if she wanted to make Derry look good to me, here, in this place. "Never got handsy when he tipped me," she said, snapping the elastic band that constituted underwear.

I set my mouth in a thin line. "Were you two a thing? Were you together?"

Destyny gave me a look, the kind a mom gives a three-year-old for refusing a peanut butter and jelly sandwich. She was, I knew without knowing, just such a mom.

"Honey, I am a professional," she said. "But not that kind of professional. Wish I knew more, but he hasn't been in for a while. Maybe not since last summer."

She glanced in a compact mirror—where had she stashed it?—and tweaked her eye shadow. She appraised me, and I sat up straighter. "Do you even wear makeup? God, I'd kill for your cheekbones."

I was wearing makeup now, but I thanked her. Like a magician, she materialized a glossy brochure and slid it across the table. "I'm a certified Face2Face consultant. I'll do your colors, free of charge, if you host a party of ten or more women. Hypoallergenic and fragrance-free."

I nodded, though I couldn't think of a list of ten women, period. I thanked her for her time and offered another five-dollar bill.

She surprised me with a hug and wished me good luck. I had never hugged a topless woman before. Her skin was slightly sticky from sweat. Also soft as a baby's.

Disheartened, I drove back to the city and ordered a burger and beer at the bar. The bartender, Cliff, was writing some kind of equation on a whiteboard. I asked him about Derry and he rolled his eyes.

"Out of tune! Every damn time he plays Blue Öyster Cult. I says to him, Derry, I says, want to borrow my electric tuner? No. He'll do it by ear. Like hell he will."

"But have you seen him?" I prodded.

Cliff paused, assessing my interest, and clammed up. "Nah," he said. "Not in weeks."

Liar. The biggest talkers never said anything. We sat, sullenly, in the windowless space illuminated by the neon glow of lottery machines. He saw me looking at the whiteboard and swiped it with a dirty rag, streaking the numbers. When the door swung open, the late-afternoon sun blinded me. In walked the faux-Derry from the grocery store, the not-Derry, the man Derry could've been had he washed his hair a bit more consistently. Styled it rakishly to convey his dedication to disinterest. The eyes were what got me, so different from Derry's brown. These were bright-blue beneath black lashes and brows. A kind of clarity. A chlorinated pool where you could drown.

He sat down beside me, ignoring all the open seats and booths. He nodded at my hamburger and bottle of beer like they were old friends.

"I think I know you," he said. He scratched his head, and his hair mussed like feathers. He was a bird. A bird that used product. The type who stared out filmy windows, puzzled by the behavior of squirrels.

"I saw you in the store," I said.

Now I had his attention. His eyes were much lighter than mine, which Derry said looked like night. His were like chlorinated pools, clear sapphire, and I recognized him finally, as one of the occasional players in Derry's band. I said so, and he frowned comically, as if to say, You caught me.

"You actually like this place?" he asked, and Cliff snorted. "We could walk around. Join me, or no?"

Can you ever know, in the moment, that there's no going back? This is what mountain climbers say on PBS specials, or cave divers, or women deciding what to do with the babies in their wombs. Maybe you know. But I would wager that hindsight is when things come clean. What all those people are talking about can't be pinpointed so accurately. They mean life. There's never any going back. Never a retreat, except in the mind. And this was just one moment: following not-Derry out into the street. Forward-ho, no going back, fine. It's just the bar, I was thinking. We can always go back.

We sat in the park, me and not-Derry, who was actually Keith. In the building across the street, a woman exited the revolving door in a smart suit and round-toed heels. She glanced at us and quickly away, hugging her large purse tight to her chest.

"Yuppie," whispered Keith. He wore an aged Dinosaur Jr. concert T-shirt that looked just like Derry's.

"Vintage?" I asked. "Or maybe eBay?"

The sky was in Keith's eyes, and I twanged down low, ovary low, inappropriate enough in the weeks following Derry's disappearance, but the body does what it wants and Keith reminded me of Derry. Keith reminded me.

"It's his," Keith said.

I went blank like a page.

"It's not my shirt," Keith said. "It's his. Derry's. I kept meaning to return it."

I stared him down. "You know where he is."

Keith shrugged. He walked to the unsanitary-looking hot dog cart on the corner and returned with two dogs and two Cokes. "He could be anywhere," Keith finally said. "Especially with a wedding coming up. What a dummy, that guy, to walk out on you. Look. His sister's hired somebody to look for him."

My face was Switzerland. On the sidewalk, a caterpillar imitated a pipe cleaner, then a camel; pipe cleaner, camel.

"And she's also hired me," he continued. "To see if you're spending out-rageously. Strippers and whatnot."

Now my face burned. He winked and pulled out a sheet with the danc-ing sleuth logo. So we were coworkers, then. He crammed the last half of the hot dog in his mouth. Poor manners, I noted. All ovary twangs ceased. He now seemed much less attractive, and much more like Derry.

"I haven't got his money," I told him.

He licked condiments off his lip and missed the ketchup. "That's too bad," he said. "He owes me. Returned my van, thank God. Picky bastard said he needed one with a trailer hitch."

"Why are you telling me this?" I asked. When he looked up at me through the fringe of dark lashes, ketchup on his lip like blood, again he had turned rakish and bad.

"I don't particularly care for my employer," he said, and smiled at me. I smiled back.

"You and me both," I said.

"Tell you the truth," he said, "I've been watching you at the bar for the last year. Unpaid position, if you know what I mean."

I knew. Twang.

After we had gone back inside the bar for more drinks, I invited him to dinner. He insisted we drive separately. In the rearview mirror, my washed-out reflection stared back. Destiny's makeup sampler card sat on the pas-senger seat, and I held it up to my face, envisioning Cheeky Apple Glow and Smoky Amethyst Eyes. Destiny's professional glamour shot was in one corner; the hot businesswoman look. I peered closer. Even backward in the mirror, I could read my Face2Face cosmetics consultant's name. For this job, she was Denise.

Our resemblance was faint. Like second cousins once removed, beneath the foundation and concealer and bronzer and eye shadow and mascara and lipstick. You had to use your imagination. You had to squint.

I watched at the window, hastily made up and perfume-spritzed, as Keith parked down the block. Five minutes later he still hadn't come inside. The rain was pouring, but I went out anyway and knocked on the window of his unmarked Crown Vic. Police auctioned, no doubt.

"It's just dinner," I said.

"I'll be back in a minute," he said, revving the engine.

He drove away, and I was miffed until he arrived with a cheap cabernet. I shut the door by pushing my body against his body. A small square condom box poked out from his jacket pocket. Maybe this was disloyal. Maybe it was being human. If someone leaves you, I thought, then it was OK for someone else to find you. I kissed him, and Keith moaned as I pushed my tongue in his mouth. He pressed one thigh between my legs and I arched against him, and he picked me up and stumbled us over to the couch.

He lay on top of me and gazed into my eyes. He brushed his lips against my collarbone, and I shivered with pleasure.

"He told me that spot was so tender you could barely stand it," Keith said.

I shivered again. This time, like when someone walks over your grave.

The doorbell rang. I pushed him off of me and stood, straightening my clothes. At the door was sopping-wet Sherryl with mud on her shoes.

"Hope I'm not too late for dessert," she said. "I've been so worried about you."

Keith, abashed, shrugged. "She's tracking me," he whispered. "Maybe later?"

My body was still warm from his body. Inside, I felt chilled.

None of us bothered with the pretense of introductions. Sherryl descended on the kitchen with take-charge maneuvering. The kind of hen who showed up in a crisis and slowly, methodically, pecked your eyes out. "Cake cutter?" she asked, opening the small white bakery box. She shook her wet locks, the curls pubic, obscene.

She lifted and plated a slice of cake. Chocolate raspberry ganache, which we had chosen for our wedding cake. *Say it*, Derry's voice commanded from inside my head. I was silent.

We sat around my coffee table, plates on knees, sobering coffee poured into mugs. Then Sherryl dropped the bomb.

"I found a note," she said.

"A suicide note," I said. My theories formed a dark new shape, tinged with inevitability.

"Not a note, exactly," she amended. "More like a map."

She pulled out a wrinkled sheet of notebook paper bearing a rough sketch, and the carbon copy of a receipt for Andrew's Tool & Die Rental. I had seen the name on Derry's credit card statement and blown it off, assuming it was for a contractor job. Sherryl explained that Derry rented a post office box. She had found the key ("Where?" "It doesn't matter.") Tons of unpaid bills. And he had mailed himself a letter, just in case. Did we know he bought property? Some land?

A hundred thousand dollars was a lot, Sherryl said, a *lot*, and while of course she cared to know what had happened to her brother, the PI was moving slow as hell, and if Derry had buried that money like he was some sort of *pirate*, damn sure she was going to dig it up. It was hers, hers and the family's. She had been forced to take matters into her own hands. In the morning, Sherryl suggested, when it was light, we would have a look. She showed me the map with Derry's handwriting. "Use her compass for exact coordinates," he had scribbled. My grandfather's compass. Sherryl asked if I recognized the spot.

"No clue," I said, which wasn't true. At the top of the page, in Derry's hand, were doodles of two flat skipping stones inked with our initials.

Sherryl began crying. She was happy. "We'll find it when it's light," she said. "We'll finally know what happened."

"What did the detective say?" I asked. I hadn't turned in a single report.

"Just deal, OK? He ran out on you. He was never who you wanted him to be."

"I never wanted him to be anybody," I said, which was true in its way. I only wanted him to be mine.

Keith had been doing a dead-on impression of wallpaper. Now he sat forward. "That's a problem," he said, and Sherryl nodded.

"You should've given him some shape, some support," she said.

"Like a bra?"

Keith's eyes darted to my breasts. I waited until he made eye contact to shake my head, almost imperceptibly. Access denied. Keith's expression was the visual equivalent of a whimper.

"Don't get smart," Sherryl said. "You think you're so smart."

Blood surged through my body. Everyone had me pegged, but I wanted to remind them: I'm not who you think I am. When would they understand?

Sherryl leaned back, spaghetti arms crossed. Keith, that dope, grabbed a slice of cake.

"Wedding cake," I said. "I won't smash it if you won't."

He held some to my lips, tentatively, and I tested it with my teeth. He did the same. "Aren't you going to eat?" I asked Sherryl.

She widened her eyes, the picture of innocence. "Was this you all's cake? Huh. I only knew it was Derry's favorite. Cost a pretty penny, too."

The map and receipt sat on the coffee table, and I studied them. I licked the cake crumbs from my fingers. The tool rental slip was wrinkled to softness, pocket-worn, and I smoothed it out on the table.

One word, typed. That's all it took to jar my mind free of fantasy scenarios. A single word typed on the carbon copy.

BACKHOE.

"I forgot napkins," I announced dumbly, retreating.

My mind spun. He had a hundred thousand dollars. He had bought land, and rented a backhoe. He had borrowed—not stolen—my grandfather's compass. What was he thinking, that he could build a house? He could barely use a table saw; I couldn't imagine him operating a backhoe. When I had tried to track him and his trail stopped cold, I fought the logical thinking: that he wasn't gone, but dead. That he hadn't left me, but all of us.

I had wanted to believe anything else. I had almost believed Sherryl. I had almost believed Keith. And when Derry and I fought, when I called him white trash over my missing sixty bucks, maybe he had believed me. He wanted to build us a house and make us a life. Later, after he disappeared, I found the money in the pocket of my jeans. I still had the crisp bills from the ATM, saved to splurge on dinner and wine when he came back. See? I would say. I should have believed you.

It's true that he lied about Denise and called me by a stripper's name during sex. It's true that he knew her real name. But to me she was Destyny. She hadn't seen Derry in the club since last summer. When we got engaged.

Sherryl and Keith were discussing plans in the other room. I slipped silently out the back door and into the rain, running barefoot on the muddy lawn, wet strands of hair slapping my neck and face. I had to look. Harder than I had been looking before. The weedy, rocky field slowed me down, but I could make out the shape of the backhoe resting on its side, the machinery slick as a fin against the sea of dark. What direction was this? Forward and backward, no compass, I saw little and could not be seen. Oh, love. Oh, love. It was never what we expected, trying to imagine a future, twining together a life with another person. We fail time and again. We ignore what's right in front of us, we ignore what's directly behind. Can't we see? We're none of us who we thought. Here lies that final truth, a stone's throw away.

Miller Miller

Nobody wanted that baby. Nobody asked that baby if he wanted to be born. And in nineteen years, when that baby had grown up and was contemplating the compositional particulars of the suicide note, those two facts weighed heavily on his mind. The baby, of course, was born nonetheless. After a mere five hours of labor, he found his way out into the world. And, due to a sixteen-year-old girl stunned dumb by the hot-slick life that had just shot out from between her legs, the child was named Miller Miller.

The nurse stood at the foot of the bed, tapping a clipboard against her hip, encased in a seafoam green scrub uniform. On her feet were crisp white sneakers, crepe-soled and silent. Stealthy.

"Name?" the nurse asked.

Lola Stephens gave the father's surname. "Miller," she said, an exhalation, the last of her labor. Tears filled her eyes at the thought of him. Jonathan Miller. Oh, Johnny. A college boy. He had gone to her high school, and denied the baby was his. He would never speak to her again, she knew. She was alone, not technically orphaned, but may as well have been, considering her disinterested parents. They had suggested extorting money from Johnny Miller for an abortion, which put an end to all the Stephens family's prenatal discussions. Lola would not keep the baby, but she wouldn't kill it, either.

"I mean the baby's name," the nurse said.

Now Lola was crying audibly, tears streaming down her young pregnancy-plumped cheeks. She looked especially childish with her two long brown braids smashed against the pillow. "Yes," she said. "Yes." It was all she could manage at the moment, the same single repeated word that last winter in Johnny Miller's rec room may have gotten her into her current situation in the first place. On a couch to the left of the ping-pong table.

The nurse had much on her mind that night. Her name was Sharon Stone (of course she was no relation to the actress, and she was tired of joking about it with patients. Couldn't they see she was *black*?) Before her shift that night, over hamburgers and french fries at McDonald's, Nurse

Stone's boyfriend of three years had asked her when she would be home. He said he had a surprise for her.

Nurse Stone wondered if he might propose. She wondered if he might announce he was cheating with another woman. Or perhaps a man. She occasionally thought about that. She was eager to be off her shift at Riverview Hospital, which was in the middle of nowhere between the upstate New York towns of Minoa and Clay. It was fall. September. The night was coming earlier and the chill was setting in, and she longed to be home in front of the fireplace with her boyfriend so she could know whether to love or hate him. Seemingly at the young woman's instruction, Nurse Stone scrawled "Miller Miller" on the birth certificate.

M iller Miller did get a middle name.
But first he was assigned a caseworker: Lydia Davenport, on the edge of thirty and still enthusiastic about her work. Lydia meant well—and tried to place him with a family that would stick—but either she had poor judgment or the system was flawed or both, and for years Miller Miller was shuffled through foster homes and paper work and adoption agencies. Lydia Davenport escorted him into each of these homes, then back out when things went wrong. With her own money, she took him out for meals and bought him candy bars and comics.

The two of them celebrated Miller Miller's fourth birthday at a burger chain. The party for two, observed by a bored teenage boy manning the counter, was a quiet affair. A yellow balloon bobbed around their heads, leaking helium. Miller Miller's most recent foster parents, Ruth and Charles Small, had often called Lydia Davenport to take the boy for a while—as if she were a babysitter. But Lydia Davenport always picked him up. Now she slurped her Coke and contemplated Miller Miller's next placement.

At first the Smalls had seemed a perfect fit. Active in their church, they frequently attended adults-only church rallies, during which Lydia would watch Miller. Later, it was discovered they were running an informal sex club in their suburban neighborhood, whereupon Miller Miller was whisked away to a nearby orphanage, examined by a doctor, and luckily found unharmed. Across the turquoise blue restaurant table, Lydia Davenport tried to ask, delicately, if he had ever seen anything that upset him at the Smalls' house. The little boy thought for a moment, setting down the purple crayon he was using to color the paper placemat.

"One time, when Puddles was peeing all over the floor, they pulled him outside by his collar. That was Not Nice."

At age seven, he landed for a time with the Tiptons, a childless farm family that introduced him to venison (and a nasty case of E. coli after eating said game) as well as a love of Big Boggle. Indeed, it was Bob and Sue Tipton, ex-hippies, who agreed that Miller Miller needed a middle name, something he could use in school or, thinking ahead (as Sue often did), in "his professional life." Sue's original thought was for a new first name as well, but Bob thought it would be too jarring for the boy. Sue always dreamed of naming a child something celestial or otherworldly, but they had passed the days when people gave their children names like Sunshine or Rainbow or Mars. Thus, they settled on Frank, after Sue's first husband.

Miller Frank Miller. The paperwork was filed.

But Frank never stuck. Miller Miller kept using only his original name, more often than not wanting both names at once. "I like how it sounds when you call me for dinner," the boy explained to his foster mother as she juiced carrots and organic honey in the Cuisinart. "'Mil-ler? Miller!'"

The Tiptons' ex-hippie blood still churned with wanderlust, though they had sold the VW bus years ago to buy a Range Rover. No hard feelings, Sue said, but they were moving to Vermont to open a branch of their whole foods market, and the new house didn't have enough room for a growing boy. They sent him to a babysitter and packed up the hundred-year-old house they had lived in for a year—the stacks of Utne Readers and the library of gardening books; the blown-glass water pipes for smoking pot that Miller Miller had always thought were vases; the cookie jar shaped like a bear that was always full of crumbly, slightly stale Oreos.

When the babysitter dropped off Miller Miller, Led Zeppelin pouring out the windows as she put-putted away in her derelict hatchback, the Tiptons were standing on the lawn talking with Lydia Davenport. Miller Miller watched as the three of them discussed how best to load the oak rolltop desk onto the waiting moving truck. His caseworker wore a tan pantsuit that had a slightly shiny look in the sun. The Tiptons, in jeans and sweatshirts, guiltily avoided Miller Miller's eyes.

"Hello again," Lydia said to the boy. It had been several months since they'd seen each other. She laid a bony arm around his equally bony shoulders, pulling the boy into the unlikely cushion of her waist.

"Don't worry," she whispered in his ear. "Somebody out there wants you."

It still wasn't Lola. As she predicted, Johnny Miller—father of the child she did not want—never spoke a word to her again. But Bruce Simcoe, another boy from high school, did. They were both twenty and had barely known each other as students back at Clay Central High. Lola and Bruce got to talking one night while working the slow six-to-close shift at Harvey's Pharmacy. Clay was big enough for a major drugstore like Harvey's, but small enough for business to be humdrum on a weeknight.

Despite the fluorescent glare above the check-out, Lola began to see Bruce in a different light. For one thing, he had clearer skin. His college tales impressed Lola. She had never been to a frat party or sat in a lecture hall, and guessed she never would. Bruce Simcoe worked at the drugstore in his red-and-blue Harvey's smock to pay for books and beer, but this was Lola's *job* job.

"Watch this," he said, and tossed a small red rubber ball marked $1.99 in front of the automatic door sensor. The door whooshed open, paused, then closed. Bruce retrieved the ball and did it again.

Lola giggled. "Pretty cool, Bruce."

He bounced the ball frenetically on the top of the checkout counter. "Remember Ashley Rawl, from our class?"

"Yeah, I guess," Lola said. In high school, Lola had never run with any group, preferring to sit on her own at lunch, reading a magazine. She did remember talk of Ashley Rawl getting pregnant, having an abortion. Was it Ashley, though? Lola was always out of the loop. Maybe the gossip was about someone else. Maybe it never happened at all.

"She broke my heart," Bruce said, with a passion that made Lola seasick. She placed one hand on the laminate counter to steady herself. "I thought I'd never get over it."

When he looked at her intently, she knew she ought to offer him a reciprocal piece about her past, a bit of her pain to balance his. But she shared with him nothing of her pregnancy four years earlier, nothing of the son she had carelessly named and discarded, even though Clay was a small enough town that he might have known, even if he didn't know the particulars. She studied each baby brought into the store, strollered or in one of those bucket seats with the straps, swaddled in blankets, held in a mother's arms. Then she peered at each face of the toddlers, and now the preschoolers. At the register, she had time to imagine her son in the bright little faces of boys who crouched to examine the candy shelf below the register, exasperating their parents with glacially slow deliberation. She would carry the habit for as long as she lived, which she felt no reason to share with Bruce. Instead she held it close, hers and hers alone.

"Sorry to hear that," she said. Bruce nodded, grateful for the words. A customer approached the register with toilet paper and Pampers.

Over time, they talked of marriage. Bruce Simcoe had caveats. One was that he wanted no children. At twenty, Lola thought that was what she wanted, too.

But somewhere in the back of her brain, Lola sometimes daydreamed about returning for her son. It would be heroic, a reunion in which crepe-paper streamers would dangle from light fixtures and they'd eat pink-icing cupcakes from Crawford's Bakery and break out in laughter, like families at the end of half-hour television sitcoms. At other times, Lola had trouble remembering the boy's name, though it usually came to her soon enough when she really wanted to think about it. Miller? Miller Miller? Why hadn't she corrected the nurse? And the few times she talked to Lydia Davenport, Lola had shut down, asking no questions about her son. She wouldn't let herself know anything about him.

She knew she would never see him again; she didn't even know where he lived. Bruce Simcoe, who after graduation continued at the pharmacy and got promoted to district manager, merely reinforced that wish. He proposed to her in aisle 7, among the candles, picture frames and other merchandise people didn't need but bought anyway. At the wedding, Lola wore white, and tried to ignore her mother boo-hooing at table 2 next to her stoic and bored father. Bruce got a little tipsy and had to be carried out of the reception hall by two of his groomsmen.

Miller Miller's own deflowering, if that's what one could call it for a boy, was more eventful than his mother's. He was sixteen. The same age as Lola when she had him.

Her name was Susie Brighthouse. People often wanted to pronounce her name Bri-thouse, but Miller Miller always said it distinctly.

"Susie Bright-House," he said that day, "did you know your eyes are more like colored glass than eyes?"

Her swan neck swiveled to face him, her blue eyes indeed like glass. She glanced away, embarrassed.

"You're weird," she said.

They were at the reservoir in Minoa, late afternoon on a school day, sitting under a maple tree, all green and red and orange leaves. They had a view of the dam where a boy from their school became brain-damaged in an accident. When he tried to slide down, his trunks caught on some stubborn, thick algae—you would think it would be smooth, slimy, allowing easy passage—and he had banged his head on the dam's concrete surface.

"Maybe I am weird," Miller Miller said.

He began pulling at Susie Bright-House's white ankle sock, the athletic kind, slightly damp. Her expensive cross-trainers sat beside her. She was on the basketball and track teams, tall, with dullish hair. Her build was always described as solid. That neck, though, defied the rest of her body.

Miller Miller was a willow of a boy, a wisp. Almost not there. He was handsome, with black eyes that looked and looked and you could never see through. His hands, as they massaged Susie's bare, calloused feet, were surprisingly strong and practiced. He was a few inches shorter than her, but she didn't seem to mind. When they lay side by side, then she on top of him, then he on top of her, height was not a factor.

It was daylight, they had no blanket, no one was around. The grass itched. They counted one another's bug bites and laughed. The empty foil condom wrapper on the grass next to them made them laugh, too. They had gotten away with something, and they were delirious. Exhilarated.

"Are you usually so prepared, Miller Miller?"

She always used his full name. He stopped laughing. He was looking at her eyes again.

"This was for you," he said. "This was only for you."

They had never completely undressed, but they straightened what needed straightening and again sat next to each other, this time even closer, looking out on the water. Miller Miller didn't hang out with the jocks or the nerds, or the kids who drank and smoked. Mostly he hung out with himself, and sometimes with one or two other guys who also fancied themselves loners. Even loners needed to be around people sometimes. Susie Bright-House's stock had been rising at their high school. She was a year older, well-liked, a good (but not too good) student. It was baffling that she would be with Miller Miller. He was incapable of being cool.

"Why did you come out here, Susie? With me, I mean."

They stared at the water rushing over the dam. It wasn't the smack to the head that caused that boy's brain damage, the doctor had said. It was being held underwater in the undertow. Fisherman found him and performed mouth-to-mouth.

"Is it true you live alone?" Susie asked.

This was information Miller Miller usually kept to himself. While he didn't take advantage of the living arrangement Lydia Davenport had set up for him, he knew other kids would. If they knew he lived in his own apartment, they would show up every weekend with their purloined six-packs, seeking refuge, pretending to be his friend. But he trusted Susie.

"Indeed," he said.

She wrinkled her eyebrows, preparing to be sad. "Where are your parents?"

"That's a good question," he said, imitating her frown.

"You mean you don't know?"

"Yup. I don't know."

Susie turned to him, and her blue eyes looked like eyes. Not like glass at all.

"I came out here with you because you asked me to," she said.

He smiled and knocked his shoulder into hers, then pushed her gently back into the grass sideways.

It often surprised Lydia Davenport that Miller Miller never asked about his parents, not even to know their names.

When he turned sixteen, Lydia worked some loopholes and set him up in his own small apartment. The unit was one of eight in a low, brown-brick building in Wellspring, a half hour from the hospital where Miller Miller had come into the world. Another caseworker from the county lived in the building, and Miller Miller was required to check in with him weekly. The landlord was a kindly older man who tried and often failed to fix leaky faucets and broken windowpanes, and he also kept an eye on Miller Miller's comings and goings.

Lydia understood Miller's parentlessness afforded him some space, room to spread out his stuff and not have to clean it up. She also knew she had misjudged on the foster homes she placed him in before, though much of it was just plain dumb luck, situations out of her hands. The apartment, she thought, provided a nice refuge as well as nearly made up for her past bungles. Why introduce unreliable parents back into a perfectly working mix?

Over the years, they had developed a bond that was less caseworker/client than sister/brother. Lydia sometimes felt closer to Miller than to her real brother, Dave, a high school principal who gave her lumpy, holiday-themed sweaters each Christmas. She visited Miller's apartment at least once a month, and sometimes more frequently, to make sure he was buying groceries and soap and all the essentials with his government assistance check. His part-time job as a video store clerk put a little extra cash in his pocket too. He sometimes repaired video game consoles at the store, and brought home an abandoned repair that no one ever claimed.

Lydia was unmarried and closing in on the end of her forties. As a caseworker, she dealt on a daily basis with a stunning array of other people's problems: drugs, STDs, hunger, mental illness. A can of mixed nuts—but the can was full of rusted nails and stripped screws, abandoned in some cobwebbed garage. Miller was one of the few exceptions. He was fairly neat, did fine in school, and seemed genuinely to like her and her company. He was the kind of client who made her feel she was doing her job, not just wasting her time on the terminally fucked. So perhaps she did visit a little more than she had to—who says you have to stop caring when the clock strikes five? Maybe she did think of him sort of like a son, though she would deny it when asked. Maybe she thought of him in other ways too, which she would also deny, to herself or anyone else.

On this visit, Miller, now eighteen, ushered her in the door like a genial host. The apartment smelled like burnt toast and oranges. Miller had started looking more man than milkweed, and Lydia had noticed he was getting his adult face. He wore a jacket that looked like a sport coat but wasn't. The heat, as usual, was turned down low. He offered her a can of soda, and they toasted with a dull clunk of aluminum. He was legally independent now, and they had arranged the visit to celebrate.

They sat on the futon couch—Lydia's old futon, which she had given him when he moved in—right in front of the TV, video game controls connecting them to the moving images on the screen. The game, as Lydia understood it, involved the senseless killing of racially stereotyped criminals in an urban setting. She loved playing. Miller always beat her, somehow easily amassing a higher body count than she could ever produce.

"What's the trick?" she asked him. "I play this game every time I'm here and I never seem to get any better."

She lit an unfiltered Camel. She knew she probably shouldn't smoke in front of Miller Miller, but surely she was the least of his bad influences between public high school and sex-addict foster parents. And when Miller indicated he would like a cigarette too, Lydia took one from the pack and lit it off her own.

"You're not putting in the necessary time," he said. "I play for hours at a stretch. You, on the other hand—" he inhaled like an expert, making it obvious this was not his first smoke, "—are inconsistent. You lack con-sis-ten-cy." He drew the word out like his English teacher, save for the puffs of smoke that followed.

Lydia leaned back on the futon, stretching her legs. Her ankle joints popped as she rotated each foot in a circle, one at a time. Her pantyhose made a swishing sound under her skirt as she moved her long legs.

"I don't care," she said.

Her tone was sullen, like a youngest child building a pre-emptive defense. She stubbed her half-smoked Camel out on the top of her soda can and dropped it in.

Miller laughed. "Sure you don't. Here, sit on the floor."

He indicated with his cigarette the space between his legs. Lydia said nothing. She pushed away the packing crate that served as a coffee table and scrambled down on the floor as Miller Miller switched the game back on, selected one-player mode, and handed Lydia the controller. He kept his hands over hers, thumb atop thumb, arms and legs encircling Lydia's upper body. The cigarette hung from the corner of his mouth. When he moved his face to the right side of Lydia's head, he narrowly avoided flicking ash in his former caseworker's hair.

"Reflex," he said, pushing down on her thumb, which in turn pushed the button on the control, making the gang member on the screen stagger back-wards in a spray of bullets.

"Hoo boy!" Lydia shouted despite herself.

Miller frowned, concentrating.

"Again," he said. "Reflex."

This time he moved forward on the futon couch, and the insides of his thighs pushed into her back, nudging her just a little.

"Sorry," he said.

Lydia didn't turn around. She wondered if he was blushing. He did that sometimes, like when he noticed the stack of sexual health pamphlets on her desk, or the time last year at the SuperCenter, when she held up a package of underwear and asked his size. Did he have a girlfriend? She knew about Susie Brighthouse, but that was two years ago and had ended painfully. Something to do with gym clothes, or his hair, or an essay in English class—there were too many things to choose from—and Lydia never got the full story from Miller. It was the principal who called her. Miller was acting out, behaving erratically, running up and down the hallways of the school in his gym uniform of gray shirt and blue shorts. It was a prank, a dare, acting stupid, he told her. But the principal said it happened after gym class, after Miller had been made fun of. While Susie didn't laugh with the other kids, she didn't not laugh. It was a snub, some sort of betrayal, and Miller never brought her up again, which made Lydia think he must have been hurt very badly.

Lydia told herself it was her job to think of these things, as if his relationship status affected her client's needs. Ex-client, she reminded herself. Then Miller pressed down on her thumb again, and a policeman on the screen shouted "No!" before falling dead in the alleyway. The pressure on her thumb felt relaxed, confident. His legs still touched her back. She jumped up suddenly, breaking the flow of the game.

"Gotta go," she said, heading towards the bathroom. "Keep playing without me."

In the closet-sized bathroom, Lydia eyed herself in the mirror above the sink as she peed. It was a tiny but neat room, with a small stack of comic books tucked neatly in a corner. You're old, she told herself. He's young. Why are you even considering this?

She *was* considering this. She must be insane. But—there was something there. She had always felt a connection with Miller. She was one of the few people who called him by his first name, who was conscious that it was a first name. In fact, she was worried that she didn't feel more lecherous. What did that say about her as a social worker?

After flushing the toilet and wrestling her pantyhose back up, she primped and fluffed her hair around her face. It made static electricity crackles and she turned on the tap and wet her hands, applying water to her hair like it was gel. The effect wasn't very effective. Through the thin plywood door, Lydia heard the grunts of urban wasteoids waylaid by nunchucks, and Miller's voice.

"Does that hurt? Does it? How 'bout this one?!"

The game replied: "Oof! Aaggh!"

She would just see what happened. It was fine. If he wanted to do it, she would. Lydia, another voice inside her said. He's 18, a senior in high school. And you're forty-seven! Jesus, Mary and fucking Joseph!

She emerged, her hair somewhat dried and her teeth given the once-over with an aggressive index finger. Miller was smoking a new cigarette, and didn't look guilty at all to have taken it from Lydia's pack on the coffee-table crate.

"Naughty, naughty," she said, her tone indicating her approval, and then some.

He shrugged, noncommittal, his black eyes flashing what seemed like anger before shifting to the floor. Lydia knew then that she had misjudged everything.

He put down the game controller. Her words still hung in the air, inappropriate and unretractable. When he spoke, he looked like he might laugh or cry or both.

"Lydia. Ms. Davenport. I think it's time I met my parents."

He said it like it was something he had waited to say his whole life, as if by turning eighteen he could finally speak the words.

Lola Simcoe, thirty-four, took her morning pill cocktail, a mixture intended to affect the reuptake inhibitors in her brain, or the serotonin levels, or something like that. She didn't quite get it. All she knew is that the pills were legal and designed to make her happy. She still worked at the pharmacy, but filled her prescription elsewhere—the SuperCenter five miles away. She liked that it was bigger, more anonymous. Most days she wore a gray hooded college sweatshirt, dwarfed in Bruce's clothing. A mouse with bags under her eyes.

Her recent diagnosis—Attention Deficit Disorder, depression, possible manic episodes—didn't shock her one bit. She was too low on the cycle for it to register. Plus, it ran in her family. Her dad was a real asshole, and though no doctor ever slapped a label on him, Lola's mother thought he was manic-depressive. So sweet Bruce talked with the doctor, explained his position (he wasn't a pharmacist, but acted with the authority of one), and coordinated Lola's pill schedule. Bruce was becoming jowly, while she appeared to shrink. He used Rogaine for his thinning hair, and a special dark tint that made him resemble Casey Kasem. Each day, Lola put her hair into a ponytail, unless she couldn't find a hair elastic. Then it just hung.

Lola snapped shut the lids of her morning pills. She used three containers of days-of-the-week pill holders, marked "morning," "noon" and "night" with a black Sharpie in Bruce's neat handwriting. "More Ning Noonan Night," she thought, a bit loopy. "What's Ning? I don't know, I just want more."

But the pills weren't working. They didn't help. Lola told Bruce that they helped, but only because he wanted so badly for it to be true. She felt the same as she always had, so there was no use in taking so many. She set one aside in her small black ring box, which was growing fuller. She shook it, held it to her ear, and when the phone rang she hid the box in her sweatshirt pocket, as if she were being observed. The same unfamiliar number registered on the Caller ID for the third day in a row. Lola ignored it again. They never left a message. Probably the doctor, who would want to talk to Bruce, anyway. She opened her binder of recipes to the hidden sheet of loose leaf paper. The note she was writing was smudged with pencil lead and erasures. She was not thinking of Bruce, only of her baby boy, Miller.

I wish we'd met, she wrote. I looked for you all the time.

She put the ring box back on the laminate kitchen table and counted the pills. Today was not the day. But soon. When she had enough pills saved. When she figured out what she wanted to write.

At the other end of those phone calls was Lydia Davenport, shame-faced and helpful, but without as much courage as she'd hoped for herself. No use leaving a message, Lydia decided each time. They never called back. She wasn't sure what to tell Miller besides "I tried." It would've been a breach of protocol to give him Lola's contact information, she rationalized.

Lydia didn't know whether a message would have helped. Lola might've returned the call. But it was no use speculating. You can't help people who don't want to be helped, and you can't reach people who never answer their phone. They never call back.

Except this time, they did. Bruce did. He found Lydia's number on the Caller ID. He was still in shock, blindsided by Lola's death, he thought she was getting better, the hang-ups and the cryptic note were mysteries he needed to solve. He read about Miller Miller's existence in his wife's shaky scrawl. Lydia tried to explain the circumstances, as best she could. Miller was away at college, she told Bruce, but she would pass on the news about Lola.

"He's doing fine," she reassured Bruce. "Better than fine."

Lydia thought about calling Miller Miller to tell him. He really was doing well at college, and she didn't want to disrupt his day. She told herself it wasn't a cop-out to mail him a copy of Lola's brief obituary instead.

Miller Miller opened the letter from Lydia Davenport in the mailroom of his dorm; seeing his social worker's name and return address on the envelope felt urgent. Inside, he found a yellow Post-It stuck to a newspaper page, on which Lydia had written:

"I found your mother. She left a note that said she wished you'd met. I'm sorry."

Her name was Lola, as the famous Barry Manilow song began. One of his foster families—he couldn't remember their names—had loved Barry Manilow. The obit listed Lola's husband and parents, no children. He didn't feel slighted. He didn't feel much at all, except relief that he didn't have to wonder anymore. Should he get in touch with Lola's parents, now that he knew who they were? Did his grandparents (!) know he existed, not far from where they lived? Did they know who his father was? He was no longer sure he wanted to know. He saw his mother's birthdate and did the math: she was sixteen when she had him.

And then he was sad. She had been so young. She wished they had met, which she took time to write down—"she left a note"—before performing an undoable act. (How did she do it? he wondered. The obit didn't list a cause of death, and even if it had, he doubted that the "how" would be included.)

Was whatever compelled her also in him? He wanted to know, he was hungry for details, and at the same time he wished he knew nothing about her at all. Maybe it was better not to know. Except: She wished they had met. That was one thing, at least, he was glad to know. Even if she hadn't found him.

"Excuse me," said the Extremely Cute Girl from the fourth floor. He wasn't stalking her or anything; he had seen her get off the elevator on the fourth floor. She smiled at Miller and squeezed past to her mailbox. He smiled back.

"Sorry, I'm kind of having an out-of-body experience right now," he said.

She nodded, eyes twinkling. "Happens to me daily."

He watched her leave. Extremely Cute Girl had an Extremely Cute Butt. From birth mom to Barry Manilow to suicide to butts? Yes. That was life, even if you wished it were otherwise. Like some kind of magician, he conjured the name of the Smalls, the couple from whose home he had been yanked as a child, their Barry Manilow records in constant rotation on the stereo. They were weirdos, he vaguely remembered. He would have to ask Lydia for the details. He held the long white envelope in his sweaty palm, smudging the ink of his name. Miller Miller, the name on his birth certificate. What was the story there? He would never know.

"Lola Simcoe," he murmured to himself, "I wish we would've met, too."

He didn't realize: they did, once.

It is summer, hot and promising, college still several months away. Miller Miller spends little time outside of Wellspring. His apartment's there, the video store where he works is there, and his high school, from which he graduated with honors two weeks prior, is there as well. The school's of little use to him now, but the video store and apartment—along with a small grocery store and gas station—make up his small, circular orbit. With the help of a guidance counselor, he's even lined up loans and scholarships and will attend Ithaca College in the fall.

Lydia Davenport has given him a car for graduation. It's a clunker, someone's tax write-off, but it will get him and his meager belongings to Ithaca where he will set up his new life. He's only driven it short distances, but today he wants to take it out, depress the gas pedal for miles at a time. Past the outskirts of Wellspring, the land offers blacktop road like stretched taffy, a way out. And later, miles later, other towns and more open roads to choose from.

He passes Minoa, where he and Susie Brighthouse rolled around on the grass at the dam. It's a small town, picturesque, a rare flatness among the hills of New York. The car manages beautifully. Lydia has done something right. Then, when he gets to Clay, he pulls over at a drugstore for some snacks and a soda. He craves Mountain Dew, something that will amplify the already-amped up emotions running through his body. Life is just beginning. College—even the sound of the word—scares and entices him. The idea of a dorm, with hundreds of people his age running up and down the long, waxy hallways. So many people. Women in nightgowns. Women in towels, walking back to their rooms from the shower.

In the store he selects the 20-ounce bottle, measuring it in his hand to make sure it will fit his new car's cupholders. He takes the drink and a bag of Cheese Doodles to the front counter, and waits patiently for the clerk to finish talking with the boss-type guy in the shirt and tie. They are discussing medicine, specific pills the man holds out in his palm. The woman puts them in her mouth, tosses back her head, swallows.

"Customer," the man says to her.

"No duh," says the woman.

Miller stifles a laugh into his fist, while the manager stalks off. Pinned to the woman's red-and-blue smock is a nametag that reads "Lola." No last name, no title. She covers her mouth with one hand, throws something away in the garbage can behind the counter. The pills? He feels a pang of concern for this woman. Wonders if he should talk to the manager. Best to stay out of it, he decides. She rings up his purchases by rote.

"Oh, hang on," Miller Miller says, and then bends over to select a candy bar from the array of goodies displayed beneath the register. She watches closely as he deliberates, eventually choosing a Mars bar. When he places it on the counter, he is startled by her scrutiny. "I'm going to pay," he says.

"I know," Lola says, then smiles. "Gotta have your chocolate, right?"

Miller Miller nods and says thanks, his eyes and mind elsewhere. Out the automated door, inside the car. Shift into gear. The road, the road, open and endless.

Locations without Maps

Marva's brother was calling, but she couldn't answer. Her cell phone vibrated in her black vinyl purse with a dull buzz, jarring her. Ringers were verboten in the test scoring facility. Answering the phone was strictly verboten. Signs on the cavernous warehouse doors said, "Deactivate phones NOW." So she had switched it from ring to vibrate, like she did every morning after entering the warehouse (7:28) and clocking in (7:30) and taking her seat at a computer in a long row of computers. About seven or eight years ago, the building had housed a discount retail store, and Marva's brother, Jarrett, had worked there as a teenager. He stocked shelves, sometimes did the register. It was one of the few jobs where he didn't receive a pink slip. He quit the store to go to college, and later quit college.

Marva had begun scoring the student aptitude tests on her computer, settling into her daily stupor, when the phone buzzed again. Her purse, next to the large black computer monitor, jumped a little across the desk. The man next to her, whose name she did not know because he wore his ID badge with the picture against his shirt and the bar code facing out (also verboten), stared at the purse as if it were a ticking bomb. They were temps; she recognized him from other projects. He was forty-five years old, a fact she learned from Sidney, the security guard, who intended to surprise her. The man could pass for late twenties, easy.

"It's just my phone," she whispered.

"Watch out," the man said harshly, his voice cracking. His hair, electrical-socket curly, reflected bluish black beneath the fluorescents. Eyes the color of milky-blue marbles darted around the room and the computer screen. If she saw him on the street instead of at the next keyboard, she might refer to him as attractive. But in here, she had learned to avoid most contact with coworkers. She had made some friends, even dated someone, but after the short projects ended—a few weeks, sometimes a few months— these relationships fizzled. She called her brother once, crying, after being stood up for coffee. When she tried to reach her new friend, a woman

76

her age who had also scored last fall's tests, she learned the phone had been disconnected.

The man next to her worked faster than anyone she had ever seen. His hand skittered across the keyboard, racking up completed test papers while he looked from Marva to the screen. "They hear that phone, you're out of here," he said. Disruption could result in an incident. You got two incidents per project, whether it was a flat tire or a ruptured spleen.

"Relax." She had a knack for calming others, even as tension knotted in her shoulders and back. She arched her neck towards the high ceiling, which in its former life had accommodated forklifts or high shelves. The walls, support beams and ceiling all were made of prickly-looking concrete. The testing facility put down thin brown carpet, then the rows of attached desks, then the computers. That was it in the way of decor.

Marva debated taking the phone outside to call Jarrett back. She knew it was him without looking at the caller ID. No one else would call—twice—before 8:00 a.m. on a Friday. She had another hour and a half before her fifteen-minute break, when she could go to the bathroom and stretch her legs. You could get up without permission, though many people raised their hands like elementary schoolers. Those brave ones who just walked out for a drink of water were observed by the workers at the rows of computers, thirty deep and fifty across, who whispered and glared at the disruption. Heads swiveling, people-watching as an excuse to break the monotony. As for unscheduled bathroom breaks, nobody said you could and nobody said you couldn't. But taking non-emergent phone calls outside of break time was unauthorized. Marva weighed in her mind whether Jarrett was emergent or non-emergent.

She didn't want to get up, not only because she wasn't up to talking to Jarrett, but because she had already had one incident, a dentist appointment, and the project was only two weeks long. Johnette, the pod's supervisor, stationed herself at the end of the row. She sucked hard candies, the only food allowed in the computer room, and made ticks next to the names on her roster. Marva had seen the penciled mark next to her own name.

The scorers handled the scanned, handwritten responses from middle school-aged children in a Western state. It tested reading aptitude. The scorers were not told the details, even though they had signed nondisclosure forms. They were not to be trusted with the information they evaluated. They weren't allowed to bring paper and pens into the scoring rooms.

Supervisors handed out pencils and erasers when the shift started and collected them five minutes before the day's end. Some temps were not allowed even those supplies, such as the young college grad in the holey red Cornell sweatshirt. He had joked that he would stick a pencil in his eye if he had to read about Timmy's bicycle, the story on the test, one more time. He had been promptly reported by another scorer. Johnette, rangy and broad-shouldered, thin as a whippet from all her break-time cigarettes, made a show of skipping his workstation during pencil distribution. The grad protested by wearing dark sunglasses inside, claiming eyestrain. The Ray-Bans made him look famous. People whispered about him as if he were. "He didn't really go to Cornell," the curly-haired man once confided to Marva. "Anyone can buy a sweatshirt."

Taking Jarrett's call probably wouldn't count as an incident, Marva thought. She could fake a trip to the bathroom. The public bathroom, rather. A few months back, she made the mistake of using the supervisor's restroom. She had sneezed violently, and with no tissues in her purse, ran to the nearest facility with her hand clapped over her nose and mouth. She was washing her hands with the designer hand soap—unlike the wall dispensers in the other women's rooms, this one had scented soap in pumps—when Johnette walked in.

"Oh, hello," Johnette feigned surprise at Marva's presence. "Listen. You have to have a purple pass to use this restroom." She held up her own purple supervisor's pass as proof. Her hands were large enough to palm a basketball.

Marva had been flustered and confused, so she apologized and explained her emergency. Johnette nodded sympathetically.

"You're a good worker, Marva Landry," she said. "Keep at it, and you'll be using this bathroom before you know it!" Marva had been embarrassed. Not only that she apologized for using the bathroom, but by the pride coloring her cheeks.

Today she didn't want to walk the distance to the all-employee restroom. She would have to pass the other workers, practically hall monitors, heads popping up like prairie dogs. She would have to traverse seemingly miles of newly carpeted warehouse, then the lobby doors, where the sign read: "PLEASE do not slam this door." She would have to keep her hand on the door handle until the click of the latch was sufficiently muted. She would have to walk outside into the cold spring Syracuse air and call Jarrett back. Jarrett who made her tired, Jarrett who made her sad.

Jarrett and the world did not mix. This was their mother's favorite subject—Jarrett and women, Jarrett and school, Jarrett and work—did he have to make it so hard on himself? Their father stayed out of it entirely, reading the newspaper in the living room while the women worked on his son. Marva's job was picking out eggshells, walking on eggshells. Trying to put Jarrett back together again after the bout of depression when he was fourteen and she was only eleven; after he dropped out of college at twenty-one. Again, now at thirty and back on unemployment, four months after losing his job at the copy shop. He was a serial job-loser. Sometimes he met women at work, but then he would get fired and forget them. Women liked him, but he didn't know what to do with their comments and flirtation. Jarrett had a handsome face—one of Marva's girlfriends back in high school said she liked his 'sexy grin,' words both true and disgusting, which consequently had burned into her brain—but it was a face that often hung with a look of sadness and confusion that Marva knew better than certain facts of her own life.

A few days ago, their mother phoned long distance, and in that breathless way announced to Marva, "Jare seems awfully down, sweets. More than usual. All these shows on TV anymore say that something like 80 percent of people are depressed." Marva and Jarrett's parents wintered down south: the North Carolina shore one year, Myrtle Beach the next. It was where they had taken family vacations. Her mother's voice and distance worked their usual magic, and Marva, at the mall buying cosmetics she didn't need with money she didn't have, had called to check up on him.

"You know you can call me any time," she had told him, only partly meaning it. She had gone to the mall to cheer herself up, to be around other people. Unlike him, she made an effort. Such as being something other than her older brother's lifeline. She resented her parents, miles away from a hundred-and-fifty-inch snow season in Syracuse, pulling her back in, snapping her out of her Cinnabon-wafted shopping reverie. She never met anyone at the mall, but sometimes she felt most comfortable in the company of strangers.

She could hear Jarrett breathing. "Yeah," he had said, hesitating. "Sometimes I just don't feel like using the phone."

He had been to doctors and psychiatrists, who found nothing wrong and advised him to take up rollerblading, to organize one corner of his home to improve energy flow, to meditate there daily gazing at his properly aligned bookshelf and dying ficus. They recommended vitamins, prescriptions, light therapy. Mostly, they told him, and later repeated to Marva and her mother in endless waiting rooms, the solution could be found in himself. It was the same thing the school psychologist said years earlier, when, defying dismal grades, Jarrett's test scores spiked to the top of the printed chart. Did he want to get better? Did he want more energy? Some suggestions worked briefly, but Jarrett's gray-shaded darkness always returned.

Marva let the call go to voice mail and turned her attention back to the screen. The tests she evaluated decided all kinds of things, the scorers were told, from funding to school programs to whether or not a kid would move on to the next grade. She evaluated the pupil's future in ten seconds and three mouse clicks. Fifty-six minutes until break.

Jarrett wanted to be better. He wanted to be motivated and hardworking and dependable. Loved, and lovable. But these were innate things, he believed, that either you were born with or you weren't. He sat in his recliner, flipping channels so fast he didn't catch more than a glimpse: *cartoon-gameshow-newsanchor-blond-dograce-basketball-blackandwhitemovie.* He only had six channels, three of which came in clearly. His thumb pressed the channel button for a couple more cycles. The phone, on the arm of the chair, sat silent, and he watched that for a moment, too. He had actually picked up the mail from the floor today after the mailman shoved it through the slot, and some of it sat on his lap, including the opened doctor bill. He thought briefly about that doctor, the redheaded one, and what she had told him last month.

He didn't know why he called Marva this morning, aside from the usual reasons he called Marva. He had already forgotten what he said, though he had left the message ten minutes before. He knew their mother had put his sister up to checking on him, and now he wanted to say something reassuring, to be the big brother for a change, even though he had never fit the role. It hardly mattered now. She was too old for a big brother. A phone call was about all he had to offer. Like a present, a piece of hope or love or whatever you wanted to call it. That he still had the ability to make contact. That he hadn't totally shut down. That he lived a static existence in this remote home by choice, which they failed to acknowledge. They wanted more.

He hadn't been back to the warehouse since he quit, a decade ago when it was the big-box store—the kind that sold dog food and apparel and tires and assembly-required furniture all under one roof. He remembered the job fondly, just about the only past job he didn't think of with shame. He worked there in high school. At night, when the store was closed and empty, illuminated only by the low-level security lighting, he would glide along the newly waxed linoleum in brown work shoes, seeing to it that the shelves were full of cartoon stationery, boxed cereal, and plastic action figures.

Once, in the fall of junior or maybe senior year, he had been in charge of setting up a display of lamps. He assembled swing-arms and desk models, tall floor lamps and overhead track lighting that hung from a recessed shelf. He screwed in light bulbs and affixed shades. Just twenty or so lamps, his supervisor had told him at the shift's start. Around 3:00 a.m., Jarrett was the only employee still on the floor, and he continued to assemble lamps. He lost count, but the pile of boxes strewn behind him formed a crumbling cardboard pyramid. He borrowed an orange extension cord from Hardware, along with a few dozen multiple-outlet surge protector strips. He went back to Hardware for more extension cords. Hours before the sun came up and the other employees clocked in, Jarrett had plugged in somewhere around one hundred lamps, but they weren't turned on yet. The cords and plugs sat in tangled heaps, and he held in one hand the master plug, the prongs sticking out of the thick orange cord.

It was going to be brilliant, a flash of summer heat lightning, or like the internally glowing glass house on the boulevard whose inhabitants didn't seem to care about electric bills. He was about to plug in the cord when suddenly the idea depressed him. It seemed wasteful, juvenile, an abuse of his earned responsibility. He began unplugging the lamps and disassembling them one by one, packing them in their original plastic and cardboard. He tried not to pop the bubble wrap. When the store opened and the fluorescent overhead lights were switched on, exactly twenty lit lamps sat on the shelves, illuminating nothing.

His family believed he had quit the job to go to college, but in truth he was scared. He had found a skill working a low-paying job. He actually liked the work, the solitary monotony of nights on the dimly lit sales floor. At age eighteen, was this his potential, so much lower than he or his parents expected? His test scores had earned him a scholarship to the university, and out of fear and obligation, he enrolled. Made it through a couple semesters.

Now Jarrett imagined his sister scoring tests in the middle of the greeting card aisle, even though he knew the place had been gutted. You needed a picture ID badge to get into the test scoring facility. It made him feel better to think of someone who might be worse off than him, even if that person was his sister. It meant a college degree equaled the same kind of shit jobs his lack of degree had delivered so far. "What's new at work?" he liked to ask, though of course nothing ever was. It was just the same day repeated, just as *his* days were the same day repeated. "Not much," Marva would admit, her peppy voice strained.

The redheaded doctor's suggestion had been simple: get out of Syracuse for awhile. Go to Florida or North Carolina, she had said. This place is tough in winter.

Could he manage a trip? He stretched in the chair, like a cat. He wore a sweatshirt and boxer shorts. His feet were cold. He didn't want to get up for socks or slippers. He didn't know if he had clean socks—probably not, then. Maybe he would drive down the street to Hardee's or to get a cup of coffee at the Mobil station, but it would mean removing himself from the recliner, dressing, searching for a hat to cover his tousled thinning hair. The newspapers were piling up on his sidewalk. He couldn't bear to face the want ads. He looked at the sleek black cordless, perched on the arm of the chair. He dialed again.

"Marva, Marva, Marva," he sighed into her voice mail. "Forget whatever I said earlier. Reason I'm calling is, you ever think maybe we don't have to be doing what we're doing? You ever think about that? Like maybe I should be the one working at that place, and you should be home, feet up, doing whatever? It's a thought."

He hung up. That wasn't right, either, but he felt like he was getting closer. He wanted lasting words, poetry, short phrases worthy of inscription on a monument. Like the brand of motivational posters that hung in offices, tying vaguely positive diatribes to single words. The mall had a kiosk of such framed posters, featuring sunsets and windsurfers in silhouette. He could crib something from Bartlett's, if he still had a Bartlett's, and recite it like an intonation. Invocation? Something. People would invite him to speak at their functions, celebrate his brilliant wit, call him a person to be reckoned with. Marva and Jarrett's father, a retired high school teacher of social studies, used to orate on a regular rotation of topics at the dinner table. "Winston Churchill said never end a sentence with a preposition." Their father repeated it each time one of his two children had done so, and Jarrett, despite his father's misinformation, still corrected his own grammar in his head. "He would be a person for whom others would reckon." "People would find that with him they would reckon." "The reckoning would be with him." His family wasn't particularly religious, and Jarrett hadn't been to church since he was a teenager, but the last version seemed biblical and wholly correct.

Outside, another gray day. Maybe winter, maybe spring. Who knew, when the temperatures were so consistently cold? The calendar said one thing, but the thermometer said another thing entirely. He had gone to the redheaded doctor with a bout of the flu. She lectured him briefly on his fruit-and-vegetable-free diet, and recommended vitamins. She asked him about his paperwork. On the form, he had checked off "depression." He didn't know if that was what it was, but he didn't know what else to call it. The doctor suggested something else: SAD.

She meant Seasonal Affective Disorder, the most aptly named illness he had heard of. AIDS aided no one, and MS made him think of braless women, circa 1972. Cancer had no initials—only that perverse hint of the positive in its first syllable. But SAD meant what it stood for. It was a disorder he could get behind, and apparently had.

A framed photo of a smiling, freckled girl playing on the beach sat atop the doctor's gunmetal gray filing cabinet. "Is that your daughter?" he asked her. He tried to hide his excitement about a diagnosis. So many others had been wrong.

"That's Molly." The doctor smiled, showing slightly crooked teeth. She handed him the picture. "She's six. That was taken on Holden Beach in North Carolina. You ought to go. It's fabulous. Lots of people winter in the Carolinas."

In the picture, little Molly was building a sandcastle, light flowing over her bare shoulders. Her whole face seemed to squint, so bright was the sun. Jarrett didn't tell the doctor that his parents were snowbirds now that his father had retired, flying south after Christmas and coming back as late as May. He didn't mention his family traveling to North Carolina when he and Marva were little. He had almost forgotten about it himself. Sunlight bleaching the wood of their rental house, with the long raised walk to the beach. The warmth of the sand on his feet, and the days when the low dunes were so hot he felt a sting and cried out, hopping down to the water as fast as he could. Those were days mandated for play, so long as he didn't bother his parents during their rest time or terrorize his little sister by splashing salt water in her eyes. Easy rules to follow.

But back home, as he grew older and more specific expectations were placed upon him, he began having what his mother termed "difficulty." Those vacations at the beach had nothing to do with finding friends or a woman or a job, or understanding himself or anyone else, or wearing a life cut from a cloth that itched against his skin.

Now Syracuse trudged towards reluctant spring. Jarrett had thought about the doctor's suggestion off and on since that appointment. What was it worth at this point, once you had gotten through December, January, February, and almost March? Survival of winter provided no comfort, only a weird pessimistic honor. He thought of a day so bright that little Molly had to scrunch her face to see the person pointing a camera at her. The day of the doctor's appointment, he had even called a travel agent for brochures. His parents stopped inviting him to the beach years before. He picked up the phone to call Marva for a third time. He finally knew what he wanted to say.

M arva sat in the cafeteria at one of the long tables covered with a red-checked vinyl tablecloth. Pictured on the glowing vending machine across from her were twelve square photos of people representing a variety of ethnicities, enjoying a host of "Hot Choice" products: burritos, jalapeño poppers, coffee. Their expressions of delight were so intense as to seem psychotic. A Hispanic man in a green turtleneck wore a white sailor cap, jauntily tilted, as if the rapturous act of eating microwaved pizza had dislodged it. Marva's clear lacquered nails tapped the table, making little ripples in her fifty-cent coffee. The poorly insulated paper cup was too full, so she had hurried it to the table, swiping the mild burn on her hand with tiny paper napkins.

Two women sat on the other side of the table and talked about their grandchildren. The one in the blue embroidered sweatshirt was a retired schoolteacher. The other, who wore jeans and a cable-knit sweater, used to be a massage therapist until she developed wrist tendonitis. "It was the only job I've ever loved," she once told Marva, swinging her long gray hair, tied in a single braid, over one shoulder. Now she affixed black Velcro supports to her wrists so she could perform eight consecutive hours of computer work each day.

Marva considered herself separate from her coworkers, a person with other goals, even if she couldn't quite give voice to them yet. She owned a condo in the city. She sometimes met friends for dinner and drinks. She was only twenty-seven, she rationalized, when the creeping anxiety about her life flooded in. She had gone to school to be a teacher but never received her state certification. Midway through the program, she realized the idea of standing in front of a classroom terrorized her. She had worked office jobs and temp positions ever since. After Jarrett, her parents were pleased that she had graduated at all. Who cared that she didn't have some Grand Plan in place, like most of her girlfriends? Each time she stepped out her own front door, each time she sipped a gin and tonic at Circ, she felt like she was living a life. She wanted that to be enough.

She listened to her voice mail. Jarrett's first two messages were nonsensical, chatty, the usual. He explained the plot of an episode of *The Flintstones*, and in the background she could hear the xylophonic scramble of Fred Flintstone's feet. He rambled about her job, and his lack thereof. She smiled slightly; it had been awhile since he had called so many times. The coffee burned her tongue. She put it down altogether when she heard the third message, his voice more controlled in tone than before: "You haven't called back yet. Stay there. We'll talk in person."

The two women at her table stood and stretched. Break was ending and Marva had barely touched her coffee. The former massage therapist smiled at her.

"You look like a ghost done scared you," the woman said. Marva couldn't remember her name, and her badge was tucked halfway inside her cardigan. Marva tried to smile, and gulped the coffee that still was too hot, scalding the roof of her mouth.

"Practically," she lisped. "Just about."

Jarrett steered the old Cutlass around the loop, and pulled onto the two-lane highway. A light drizzle fell, threatened to turn to ice on the pavement. He hadn't been out of the house in at least three weeks. He felt free, a little scared. His family protested when he had moved out of the city into a neighboring suburb two years ago, and then even farther away, into the countryside beyond the suburb. They continued to pay his rent, though, for the small ranch with a dirt lawn and a dilapidated garage he couldn't park in. In which he was unable to park. His family thought he courted isolation, even though it made him antsy. He saw it as spreading his wings, even if he wasn't going to fly.

He didn't have a cell phone, so his sister couldn't call him to say, "Don't come. *You* stay there." Jarrett chuckled as he pictured Marva's reaction to his message. She would be surprised, maybe even a little put out that he was interrupting work. But she hated that job. He knew that once he talked to her, she would be up for a change.

His last job was in the city, at the copy shop, and he had had a long wintry drive each morning and night. It was almost pitch-black by 5:30 p.m. He stopped going. If it was still dark when he woke in the morning, or even at night, he would shut his eyes in bed until he could see some light through his eyelids. His boss was right to fire him, though Jarrett preferred to think he chose to stay home.

The highway cut through a mix of farms. Coming up on the right, the Baptist church had a new roof and a large addition attached to one side. It looked cheaply made—shoddy work and materials. The last time he drove by, construction had not yet started. The message board, close to the highway and across the short lawn, announced "Best vitamin for a Christian? B-1."

Closer to the city, the low grim buildings and wet streets took over the landscape. Water splashed against the car's wheel wells, a mechanical shushing noise. He took a shortcut through his parents' neighborhood, to the house where he and Marva had grown up. In winters it was empty and would smell of cold disuse. Marva house-sat; he had never been asked to. The house had four bedrooms upstairs, but at age thirteen he had moved himself down to the windowless basement. He slept on the recreation room's fold-out couch. He read fantasy novels and played video games, inhaling the earthy scent of the root vegetables that his mother kept in bins, in a small closet next to the slotted wooden staircase. Even with his door closed he could smell them, the potatoes and carrots and onions and dirt, or at least imagine he could.

Back at her desk, Marva was clicking almost as fast as the man next to her, barely needing to read the tests, when she came to one that made her pause. The question asked pupils to explain what happened in the story they were required to read, about a boy named Timmy who learned how to ride a bike after repeated tries. She rechecked it to be sure it corresponded to the right question. In neat, precise penmanship, the child had written:

I know he was scared, but Timmy should ride the bike sooner. I get scared too. I feel sad every day.

Marva's eyes turned unfocused, moving away from the test that she could only give one point out of six (for mention of Timmy and the bike.) Had Jarrett felt this way, this young? She couldn't remember. His depression wasn't on her radar until a vacation to the North Carolina shore, when Jarrett was a freshman in high school and Marva was still at the junior high. That was the last year they went, and they had planned to stay two weeks. In the middle of the trip, Jarrett locked himself in his room for an entire day and night and refused to talk to anyone. First they tried reasoning with him. Then her father yelled that he would break down the door. Her mother was convinced that if they left him alone, he would want to come out eventually. Later, she secretly sent Marva back to Jarrett's door with a juice glass to press to the wood. "I hear him breathing," she reported. That satisfied her mother, who went downstairs, maybe opened some wine.

But Marva stayed outside the door all night. Jarrett nudged her head with his big toe when morning came. The first thing she saw when she woke up was the sand crusted under his thick, yellow toenail. She looked up at her big brother from her spot on the Berber carpet, and he barely seemed to see her. They left North Carolina five days early, their father fuming behind the wheel. Their parents asked repeatedly: What was he doing? What was he thinking? Jarrett never told them. About that, or anything, really. It wasn't until they crossed the Pennsylvania state line that he started talking to them again. He said Marva's sun-streaked hair was very Bride-of-Frankenstein. He requested they stop for burgers. He acted like nothing had happened. So it hadn't—it just disappeared. But Marva remembered.

The sound of the seldom-used intercom crackled overhead. Sidney, the security guard, cleared his throat into the microphone. It was a distinct, phlegmy sound; anyone who had worked a project had heard it before in the lobby as he greeted people.

"Excuse the interruption."

The key-and-mouse sounds faded, followed by a rising hum in the air. Marva ducked towards her keyboard, in contrast to the other workers whose heads swiveled.

"Marva Landry, you have a visitor at the front desk. Marva Landry."

A second voice, Jarrett's, came through before Sidney turned off the mic: "Say it's urgent."

Next to Marva, the rapid scorer put a hand to his mouth. His curly black hair shook a little. "Uh-oh," he said. His eyes widened. He had just spent ten minutes conferring with Johnette, agonizing over whether a test should get four points or five. For the first time in a long time, Marva wanted to walk out and never return.

"Grow up," Marva said. She grabbed his shirt and flipped over the attached badge. "William."

He nodded and turned back to the screen, eyes still darting, hand still clicking the mouse. He whistled a tuneless dirge through his teeth. "Been nice working with you."

"Has it?" she asked, biting off each word. "Do you even know my name?"

William's eyes focused on her, finally, and softened at the corners. He pointed skyward to the intercom speakers. "Marva Landry," he said.

She stood and squared her shoulders, ignoring the low rumbling voices around her. Her black-heeled boots trod silently on thin carpet, permission to leave granted. Johnette pointedly looked at her wristwatch, her pencil poised over the roster.

When his sister appeared in the lobby, Jarrett calmed immediately, and smiled to offset the annoyance and agitation he knew to expect. The security guard watched them with interest.

"Let's go outside," Marva said, and he followed instructions as usual.

A wide parking lot separated the warehouse from the street; traffic whizzed by, semidistant. They each breathed in the clean-smelling air.

"So what brings this pleasant surprise?" Marva asked, and sounded like she meant it, mostly.

"Boy, this place looks different," he said. "You think I shouldn't have come, huh?"

Marva gave a small shrug and sort-of smiled. The building had a dirty film on the storefront windows; cigarette butts littered the curb. He pointed to the windows. "When I worked here, you wouldn't see that. I'd be on a ladder with a squeegee, you can bet. I was great with the squeegee. In fact, they let me do damn near everything around here."

He licked his lips. "Listen, Marva. Listen." He held on to his idea for a moment longer, wanting to savor it before sending it into the world. "We can be halfway there by nighttime."

Marva tilted her head to one side. "Halfway where?"

"We're going to North Carolina," he said. "Doctor's orders." Jarrett grinned, feeling the sweat that beaded on his upper lip and at his temples. The wind kicked up his hair, already cowlicked. Absentmindedly, his sister reached up to smooth it, and he ducked her hand.

"The last doctor I saw knows what my problem is, and it's *here*. Look at this parking lot, look at this street! Everything's damp. And when it's not damp, it's frozen. It's like, look at pavement, right? And potholes. That's what winter does. Gets inside your cracks, you know? There's no reason we have to stay. We can just go. So let's go."

Marva seemed to appraise him, a little glimmer of excitement in the corner of her mouth. He didn't know if it was towards him or his plan. He would take either one.

"Have you talked to Mom and Dad?" she asked, and Jarrett's hope deflated. Same old responsible, practical, dead-end Marva. He wasn't going to be dead-end. There were unmarked avenues and highways inside him, locations without maps.

"I'm going," Jarrett said. "I'm driving all night to North Carolina. I'll get a cooler, stock up on sandwiches and drinks, and I'll barely have to stop. Maybe stop a couple times, but only when I have to. I might stay at that old campground in Virginia. I haven't decided. So you can come or not come. I'm going either way."

Was that really true? He wasn't sure, but Marva looked impressed. When they were younger, those beach trips had been the highlight of each summer, the whole year. He knew he'd ruined it the last time, though he couldn't understand why his parents were so upset. He couldn't explain his behavior, which made them angriest. Nothing in particular set him off; this was how he was. *Who* he was. Couldn't they let him be? Let him exist, on whatever side of the bedroom door he chose? He knew Marva had blamed him all those years ago for the lost vacation. He could make it up to her.

"So what do you say?" he asked.

"I've got to finish this project or they won't hire me back," she said.

"Big deal! They'd be doing you a favor."

She was quiet a moment. "I *want* to work here. I *want* to have a job."

The toes of his old sneakers were scuffed. He could not remember how old these shoes were, or where he had bought them. Marva patted his shoulder, and he startled to attention. "I'm sorry," she said. "I've got to get back inside." She glanced back while pushing open the glass door to the building. "I really am sorry, Jare. But hey—go down there. It would be good for you."

He watched her through the glass, nodding to the security guard as she walked back into the scoring room. When the guard turned his back to rummage through the mini-fridge, Jarrett strode through both sets of doors as if he still worked in this building. He stood alone, taking in the room. Marva started towards him, terror on her face, but he jogged away, down a row of computers. A tall woman called after Marva, perturbed. "Hey," she said, her teeth clunking hard candy.

"This is where the registers were." Heads popped up at the sound of Jarrett's voice, which echoed in the quiet room.

He indicated a large bank of computers with sweeping hands. "You guys would have been children's wear." A few people, the ones who remembered the store that once occupied the warehouse space, chuckled. Jarrett took off down another aisle. The security guard had entered the room, walkie-talkie pressed to his mouth, walking fast.

"Bikes. Candy. Tools." Jarrett paused by a pillar and picked up the white telephone still attached. His voice came over the intercom. "Associate to Housewares. It still works!"

Some of the employees laughed, others were perplexed, and a few continued to score tests. The guy in the Cornell sweatshirt and sunglasses raised one red arm like a flag, fist clenched in salute. A woman who had to be Marva's supervisor stood with her arms crossed, a referee waiting to call the play.

"I'm sorry, Sidney," Marva hissed to the security guard. "It's just my brother. He's harmless." Sidney lifted his hands, one of which had rested on the gun tucked in his belt holster. Good God, Jarrett thought, sudden fear coursing through his body, what did I do? Were standardized tests that important? Or was it the employees he was protecting?

Jarrett turned slowly to face his sister. In her voice and face she showed her burden. It was him. Marva looked like a dog kicked by its owner, eyes full of pain and questions, and yes, love. Even that. Even now. He slumped into the single chair left in a row of empty cubicles, exhausted. What had he been thinking? He could barely make it out of the house; how would he drive alone to North Carolina? Marva knelt down and put a hand on his arm. They stayed like that a long time. People lost interest and went back to work. The room filled with the sound of soft caresses of keyboards, mouse-clicks.

"When I worked here, it was a great job," he said, so softly she had to bend closer. "I worked nights. Once I had to put together all these lamps."

"Yeah?" she asked. It took Marva a minute to maneuver to the ground, then to arrange her heeled boots in a cross-legged position. A few strands of gray hair sprung from the part in her dark hair; unnoticeable unless you were looking down from above, as he was. Oh Marva, he thought but did not say, thank you. He could've wept with relief. Just like that year at the beach, when he had finally unlocked his bedroom door and found her sleeping on the hallway floor. To be needed was a beautiful thing. Now he bit back tears in the test scoring facility. She looked up at him like a baby bird, waiting to be fed. He didn't know where to start, only that he would, here, in an empty aisle he had once filled with unlit lamps.

Where Light Can't Reach

The boys and I were at loose ends by the second week of winter break, our travel canceled and future on hold. We had played with Christmas presents and assembled robot kits and complicated model cars, and set up puzzle tables and baked so many cookies we couldn't consider eating another, no way, then ate three more and rubbed our bellies, groaning. Frank had left the day after Christmas to be with his parents, and I'd been alone with the kids for the last two weeks. My father-in-law, Frank's dad, was ill. Cancer. And now a broken hip on top of that. My husband was a good son, volunteering to convert the outside stairs of his childhood home into a ramp for his dad. I could hardly begrudge that he hadn't done any of the gift wrapping or shopping or baking or meal prep, and that his present to me had been a gift card to the mall, as generic as they come. He was stressed about Pop. We all were.

Mom? our younger boy called from downstairs.

Yes? I answered, but he didn't respond.

My own family was back in Boston, wondering why I didn't just put the boys in the backseat and come home already. I hedged, and Frank asked what I was waiting for. He was guilt-ridden that it had been so long since we'd seen my own healthy parents and sisters and large extended family, the dining table a mess of cloth napkins and dessert plates at the end of holiday dinners. But I wanted to be ready to drive to his folks' place if summoned. And, I was a little relieved to opt out of holiday travel: it's hard to muster fake cheer at Christmas. Everyone noticed the tiniest hint of grimness and policed your behavior accordingly, as if a cup of eggnog might be the thing to lift the corners of your mouth. Maybe spiked? No? How about another wedge of sausage-breakfast quiche?

My family was loving. My family was relentless. What's wrong? they would ask when I wasn't careful with the look on my face. This year, I was glad they wouldn't have Frank and me under a microscope, noting whether he sat on the far end of the couch, or if I avoided eye contact when he complained about how challenging it was to raise kids. He meant the forming of their moral centers, not the daily tasks that mostly fell to me: buying sneakers and school clothes, making and keeping doctors' appointments and playdates, slicing grapes lengthwise, plating sandwiches with crusts I refused to cut off and the boys refused to eat, leaving behind Tetris-like pieces, a stalemate in a game that couldn't be won.

Oh Francis, that girl had messaged him, You seem like *such* a good dad. I swoon.

Nobody called him Francis. But we couldn't talk about that now. I was busy with my little family: me and my two boys. And Frank, of course, who had said nothing of my visiting or coming to help, Frank who was several hours away in northern Indiana. It seemed farther.

Mom? My younger son called again.

What? I yelled back.

Just wondering where you were, he said. Yeesh.

While I sat at the computer, fidgety, the boys were downstairs, arguing over a board game. I was late in prepping my adult education Spanish classes at the Community Center. Before the boys were born, I taught high school and ran the Spanish club, arranging outings to Mexican restaurants, and movie nights featuring Spanish and Argentinian films. I missed my classroom and my students, and questions lived in my mind: Were the kids old enough to need me less? Could we manage if I went back to work? We were getting closer to yes when Frank's dad was diagnosed. It wasn't the time to make a change.

I could hear the kids through the floor vents as I worked: The eight-year-old said his little brother's new Spider-Man coloring book was for babies, and judging by the scream, that strong little six-year-old punched him in the arm. Then both were crying. I knew this scene would repeat throughout the day. It was nearly impossible to keep a lesson plan, or even a thought, in my head, so I saved and closed the mostly blank document of Spanish idioms. And then the boys were silent, as if my defeat had been their goal. Maybe they had called a truce. Or knocked each other unconscious.

We needed some distance. No one wanted to be home any longer, cloistered in the dry air of a house that needed a humidifier. Our hair and clothes crackled, our faces were tight and dry. Pricing out a humidifier was a Frank job, and Frank was not home. I would take them to the park, for a drive, anything. I reached into the closet for my down vest, moving aside my old camera case collecting dust on the shelf.

What's that, mama? my oldest asked, startling me.

I set it on the desk and carefully unzipped the cracked leather case. The noise drew my youngest, materializing at my elbow. The boys peered inside at several rolls of unused film, along with my old camera. The film was at least twenty years old and probably no good. Still, I wanted to show the boys how this artifact from another life worked. I displayed the film canister in my palm, and the younger one gazed at it, transfixed. How do you put that thing on Facebook? he asked, and I laughed.

Bro, his older brother reprimanded. You don't even have a Facebook.

Let me show you, I said.

Now I was the age of people who said *In my day*. I explained the lens and light exposure, and developing prints in the darkroom with photo paper. The chemicals, the water bath. I had a nice SLR camera and a point-and-shoot, and I picked the latter to show them how to load the film into the camera. I added fresh batteries, snapped the back shut, and the film automatically wound around the reels and advanced to the first frame.

Show me again, said my impulsive younger boy, reaching to open it. I grabbed his hand. His nails needed clipping, which I had overlooked after his last bath. Sunday? Maybe longer.

No, you can't expose the film to light, or it gets ruined, I explained. You have to keep it shut until after you take the pictures, then the film winds back up in the canister, where light can't reach.

Like a secret, said my older boy. His dark eyes, button nose, and shrewd demeanor sometimes reminded me of a fox.

Exactly, I said, wondering what secrets lived in my eight-year-old's heart. He didn't have a Facebook either. But his father did.

We packed up the camera and gear, the January day unseasonably warm, and the sun felt bright only because it had been gone for so long. It trickled through tree branches, pale as egg whites. At the drive-through I ordered cake pops and a large coffee for me. Drivers waved one another through the intersection, the weather perking everyone up. It had been a while since I'd seen the three-part Hoosier wave: 1. You may get into my lane. 2. Thank you for letting me into your lane. 3. No problem, my lane is your lane. It was once native to Indiana but had grown rare. I pointed it out to Frank, born and raised here, who said he never really noticed. I remembered his words: That's just what you do.

We headed eastward to a small town about forty minutes away. The sun made the rutted farm fields glisten; they were fallow and muddy, with shiny patches of old snow melting into the tractor tracks. Frank and I had driven this route many times before having kids, when we had the luxury of time and ways to spend it. On the town square was an Italian restaurant run by two brothers, who we privately called Primo and Secondo, after characters in the movie *Big Night*. One looked a tiny bit like Stanley Tucci, the other had none of the temperamental attitude of Tony Shalhoub's perfectionist chef. These two were second generation, their English perfect, and they loved the Colts and Pacers. Signed photos of professional athletes who had visited the restaurant hung on every wall. Nicknaming the pair was our private conversation, mine and Frank's, a game of pointing out to one another the ways that life was like its film reproduction. Today the sign on the door was flipped to "Closed," though it was after lunch. I pulled over and took a quick picture of the restaurant with my phone.

Mom? Don't you want to use the camera? The boys had been using it to snap photos out the window.

Let's save some for the park, I told my older son. They were used to unlimited digital shots, my oldest especially, borrowing our phones to shoot pictures of cardinals at the birdfeeder, or to make stop-motion videos of LEGO adventures. He rewatched them with a tiny smile on his face.

He had been most attuned, lately, to the petty arguing Frank and I had tried to hide, asking me once if "separation" was as bad as "divorce." Where'd you hear that? I asked, panicked, wondering if Frank had uttered those words, which I had never said, to Frank or the children. The bus, he said, waving vaguely out the window, weary of the subject.

When Frank's father was diagnosed—the word "aggressive" used for both the sickness and the treatment—our energy for bickering drained away. The boys were distraught about Pop. So was Frank. We all were. Frank and I abruptly shifted focus, no longer passive-aggressively commenting on who had last emptied the dishwasher or signed the kids' homework logs. We were laser-focused on Pop and his treatment plan. It was the only thing Frank could talk about, which I understood. And though I refrained from bringing it up, I was unsatisfied with his dismissal of the recent string of Facebook messages to that girl he had known in high school. No big deal, he claimed, though the paragraphs of their conversation scrolled at length down the screen. Really, Francis? I thought but did not say.

At the park I sat on a bench while the kids scaled the jungle gym and climbed giant tractor tires half-embedded in the ground. My most comfortable college sweatshirt made me toasty, INDIANA in block white letters on red, and I unsnapped the down vest layered on top. I was wearing this sweatshirt when I met Frank, standing in line at the campus Big Apple Bagels, which quelled my homesickness for the East Coast. Soon it was Frank, and Frank's tech job, that made me comfortable here, not quite a thousand miles from my family in Boston.

I used my phone to take a picture of the boys, then took another one using the film camera. A footbridge over a stream had the careful, honed look of an Eagle Scout project, and two young boys near my own kids' ages stood looking down at the shells and rocks below. Their mother watched from the opposite bank, wearing a thin blue hoodie and smoking what looked like an e-cigarette. We waved to each other but kept our distance. My two ran over, and the four began playing together, fast and instant friends animating the empty swings and teeter totter.

Woot! they took turns yelling, a spontaneous call-and-response game they invented on the spot, a single syllable made of joy.

I texted the picture of our children to Frank. He replied instantly: I miss them! Which park?

I added the restaurant picture as geolocation. He sent back a heart emoji, and a line from the movie: "Sometimes the spaghetti likes to be alone." I laughed out loud, nobody near enough to notice. Before kids, before the house and yard, we would spend Saturdays watching movies on the old pullout sofa bed in our apartment. "Oh Marie," he would serenade me along with the Louis Prima song from the *Big Night* soundtrack, though that wasn't my name. Now I felt myself tearing up and slid on my sunglasses. The messages he sent that girl—a woman now, but she had been a girl then, and was probably still that girl in his imagination—weren't even flirtatious; that was the worst part. They wrote each other thoughtful notes about their parents' health, about nineties bands on comeback tours, about the governor's bungling of the HIV crisis in southern Indiana. He offered a solution to fix her glitchy laptop. They shared memes with references I didn't get. They had once been connected, and now were reconnected, and I felt slighted, shut out of my husband's life. Our conversations at home, when they weren't about Frank's dad, centered around the logistics of the kids' baseball and hockey schedules, parent–teacher conferences, what was for dinner and whether it was something the kids would eat. It was exhausting and repetitive. It was life.

The week before Frank left for his parents' house, I had accidentally read the messages. She addressed him as Francis. She wrote, I've always loved your folks, Francis, and I'm praying for the best possible outcome for your dad. Such a sweet man, just like his son. Frank's laptop was open on the couch, unhidden. Francis? I said, my voice all uptalking sarcasm, which was a mask for jealousy, which was a mask for fear. He laughed. It's sort of an inside joke, he said. From that old movie *Stripes*, where the guy named Francis doesn't want to be called Francis? That was my nickname in marching band. I shook my head, went to get a snack from the kitchen, even though I wasn't hungry. Your nickname is Frank, I said over my shoulder.

He was named after his dad, who also went by Frank. My husband was Frankie, but only to his family. Sometimes his dad called him Junior, and he barely referred to me at all, a woman with too many opinions for his liking. I would not describe him as sweet. Two Christmases ago, I overheard him telling my husband that he ought to get a handle on me and my mouth before it was too late. My Frank told his dad, That's hardly necessary, and she's not a horse.

We had argued about his dad in the car later, his sexism and traditionalism, until we realized that our wide-eyed boys were listening to every word. We lapsed into silence. The kids finally fell asleep. I wanted to say more but was still too heated, unable to fully appreciate my husband's defense. Frank broke the tension with an incredibly accurate horse whinny and snort. We woke the boys with our laughter. They snorted and neighed along with us, delighted, with no idea why their family had turned equine.

Across the park, my younger son piped up, What's your name? His voice carried across playgrounds, grocery store aisles and mall corridors, and up and down our street as he rode his little bike, newly without training wheels. We joked that he had two volumes: on and off. I couldn't hear his new friend's reply, but moments later my son was summoning me over. He raised his eyebrows and widened his blue eyes, which he did when he was in charm mode. Really, charm mode was his natural state. He wanted the camera so he could take a portrait of the others. It's a film camera, I explained to the boys' mother, who warily watched the photo op. We could send you a copy. Her boys stood tall and proud, used to being the smiling subject of somebody's photos.

Say cheddar, said my child, aiming the camera and clicking.

She shook her head. I'm just their aunt, she said, as if that explained something. Abruptly she called out, Tommy, Brad, time to go home. She pointed to the new housing development visible beyond a small patch of woods, and the boys trotted after her. We waved goodbye. My two resumed shell collecting along the creek banks, and I took a few more photos of them posing with their treasures.

We approached the hill to the parking lot in sweeping cutbacks, not because it was that steep, but to pass the time. So many of my parenting maneuvers involved trying to wear the boys out, and usually I wore myself out in the process. Today I felt strong, energetic, powered by the sunshine. Wasn't that nice, I asked, to find new kids to play with?

Yeah, but I wish they could've stayed longer, my oldest said. Why did their mom make them leave?

Aunt, I corrected automatically, but what did it matter? I liked correctness and facts, and being right, which my mother had chided would not serve me well. Better to pretend you don't know some things, she once said, out of earshot of my father and Frank, after a dinner-table debate about I no longer remember what. It's easier for wives that way.

Maybe Tommy and Brad are going to have lunch, I said.

It's too late for lunch, my youngest said. We ate lunch already. Also? I am sick of PB&J sandwiches. In case I didn't tell you before.

My oldest's forehead crinkled. Mom? Those aren't their names. Their names are Brady and Oliver.

A chill ran through me and I glanced over my shoulder, expecting to see them looming. But there were toddlers and parents playing in the park now. The boys and their aunt were nowhere to be seen.

My two children waited for my ruling on the matter. I shrugged, and on the pavement my shadow copied the motion, puffy down vest rising and falling. The boys' collected shells clinked deep in my pockets.

Maybe they have nicknames, I finally suggested.

Exactly, my younger child agreed. Like how people call me Captain Awesome.

No one calls you that, his brother said.

I call myself that.

Fair enough, I said, unlocking the car. On the way out of town, the Italian restaurant on the square was still closed. I miss Daddy, said the six-year-old, out of the blue. I know you do, I said. My oldest was silent for most of the ride home, while his brother shot the remaining film exposures. Look, an AutoZone! *Snap*. Nobody did one-hour photo developing anymore, they mailed it out, and at the drugstore near our house, I printed my name and address on the envelope for the clerk, who said it would take two weeks, minimum. Even though we were five minutes from home, we bought bottled water and snacks, and I relented and allowed two rubber snakes onto the counter.

This is going to be so cool, I assured them, but the boys were tired of this adventure, tired of my attempts at cheer. They wanted to go home and watch TV, or space out on their tablets, or read a comic book. They wanted to make their nightly video call to their dad, while I stood in the hallway outside their bedroom, folding towels and matching socks. Won't it be neat to see when the pictures are developed? I tried again.

No offense, but it would be better to see them now, the older one said.

Yeah, said his brother, a tiny crony.

I wonder if Brady and Oliver are allowed to play *Fortnite*, the older one mused, watching me for a reaction. Not just about the video game, forbidden at our house, but the names he had chosen to use. I did not correct him, only nodded to show that I'd heard.

Once the kids were in bed, I poured myself a glass of wine and collapsed on the couch. Frank's tablet on the bookshelf dinged, and I automatically stood and crossed the room to turn it off. Notifications flickered across the screen as I muted the volume. His tablet was still logged in to all of his accounts. I should not have been looking. But I had to know: was he still talking to the girl, the one back home who was so fond of his parents? I tapped the icon, and the conversation appeared. They had arranged to have coffee, or more precisely, they had already had coffee, around the same time the kids and I were driving back home. The last message in the string came from her: So incredible to see you again. Here's the picture I was talking about. She included a snapshot from high school of the two of them sitting on the trunk of a 1990s-model Ford Taurus, arms slung across shoulders.

My stomach dropped. I should not have looked. I wanted to delete the photo, a moment captured by light sent through a camera years ago, now made digital, pixels reforming an image in the far-off future, which was now. I did not delete the photo. Instead I navigated to the home page, scrolling Facebook as if to cleanse my brain. How disorienting to see Frank's feed instead of my own. It appeared more uplifting, more photogenic, than mine. Judging from the pictures, many people had enjoyed the beautiful day. The exercise influencers took their complicated lose-the-holiday-pounds routines outside (*Subscribe for more!*), followed by a complimentary smoothie recipe. Frank's mother had posted a meme-like prayer for healing the sick. "You liked this" the screen said, meaning Frank had. Long threads of other people's conversations were devoted to the plot of a new television show, replays of NBA games, holiday recipes. The nagging feeling in the back of my brain dulled to a low ache.

Until I saw the kids from the park. On any other day, I would have scrolled past the post shared by one of Frank's coworkers, featuring side-by-side school pictures of the two boys my children befriended, several years younger but clearly recognizable in T-shirts and gap-toothed grins, on a crudely fashioned "Missing" poster. It had been shared a few hundred times, the original post written by a man with a stone-faced profile photo, his eyes hard and flat as old pennies. Boys need a father in their lives, he wrote. I miss Ollie and Brady so much. Their mother needs to let me see them NOW.

It wasn't a news story or police report, or anything remotely official. That's what set me off: this Microsoft Paint fabrication of their absence, with the word "Missing" in bloodred. My protective hackles rose, the deepest, truest feeling I knew, radiating outward from the marrow of my bones. Maybe this father did not deserve to see the boys. Maybe they were with their custodial parent, a mother who was willing to say she was just an aunt. Who had thought, anticipating recognition or retribution, to change their names. Their father did not have their most recent school photos. If the boys had been in danger, they no longer were, I decided without evidence. It felt true.

I began typing immediately. If I had paused, or tried to reason with myself, I might've backspaced. But the words needed to come out.

The boys are awfully happy without you. What did you do to make her want to leave?

I could see the rippling dots that indicated someone was typing a response, and I waited, almost gleeful. I had said the thing that I hadn't known I wanted to say. I felt an almost cathartic release. Then the message popped up below mine, from a woman wearing an American flag T-shirt in her profile photo:

Who are you, Frank? When and where did you see the boys?

I was still cloaked in Frank's account, feeling anonymous, and now I was dizzy with adrenaline and confusion. If I wasn't logged in as my husband, I never would have seen these boys again. I never would have engaged with a stranger about two children I did not know, not in any significant way, whose lives had chanced to intersect with ours for less than an hour of a single afternoon. Yet I had acted instinctively, and it felt right until it didn't. I stabbed at the screen to delete the comment, which had already garnered five "likes," and turned off Frank's tablet. My heart pounded in my ears, my face flushed. I got up and closed the drapes, the squeak of curtain rings on the metal rod as loud as my conscience.

Later, in bed, my phone buzzed with Frank's good-night text. Thx for park pics, he wrote. Good day overall? I got a break from house & parents & grabbed coffee with an old friend.

I replied, The one who calls you Francis?

He sent back a crystal ball emoji to indicate my psychic power. Yes, she and her partner both call me that! Btw, were the kids using my tablet? I got weird notifications on my phone.

I don't know, I replied. I'll check.

No worries. Thanks, love.

The ache I had felt earlier dissipated, though the foolish shame from reading his messages did not. It was as if I wanted to find something damning. When I suspected his betrayal, I had the thought: what if I took the boys to Boston? What if we stayed? It was the briefest, momentary flicker of an idea, a fight-or-flight response, and I didn't want to fight. I wanted to hurt him back. I wanted a reason to act. I was almost physically sick imagining how sad Frank would be without the boys. And without me, I supposed, though I had my doubts, seeded in me the way a dark cloud is seeded with rain. Maybe my mother was right: it was better to pretend you didn't know some things, especially the things you weren't meant to see. I reminded myself that the tallying of daily grievances and emails with an old friend were not enough to prompt interstate flight. You did not make the big gesture until you had to. Until it was urgent. Like the woman in the park, Ollie and Brady's mom. There was a difference between real danger and the kind you invented.

I couldn't sleep. Downstairs, Frank's tablet was plugged into the wall charger. I turned it on, returning to my husband's Facebook account and dreading the fallout from my now-deleted comment, but there was nothing new other than a private message, and I felt a wave of relief to have disconnected my husband from the mess I had made. I touched the screen to access my husband's in-box, expecting to find another gushing note from his high school friend, the one with a partner, as if that defined or settled a person's status. But it was from the stone-faced father, whose name was Rod, and I was glad the drapes were closed when I read his message:

I know where u live

Fear pricked at the back of my neck as I tried to rationalize that this statement couldn't possibly be true. I knew Frank was asleep and had not seen the message yet. I deleted it and blocked Rod. What were the odds that a stranger would come to the house over an online comment? Slim to none. Nonexistent, even. Still, I double-checked the locks and pulled out the sofa bed so I could sleep downstairs, acting as a sentry between my boys and the world. What would I do, alone with two small children, if an angry man came into the house? I wished Frank were home, and not because I missed him. I banished the thought just as I had the online messages: delete delete delete. The springs of the old sofa bed mattress poked into my spine no matter where I lay.

With the kids back to school and my classes starting in a week, I had nearly forgotten about the film developing until I received a call that the order was ready. At the drugstore, I picked up a bottle of wine and a package of cookies. Tonight Frank was coming home, surely exhausted from his time at his parents.' I tried and failed to picture our reunion, and what we would talk about. Would we hug and kiss? On the cheek or the lips? In front of the kids? I wanted a script, I wanted the movie filmed and available on DVD so that years from now, we could watch it together on the couch. I wanted to know my lines, my cues.

What do you do with the things you weren't meant to see and weren't supposed to say? How do you make a long life together, leaving room for all the people who would be in it? I was really asking, How do you get through a day, and then another, and another? There was no script.

I waited until the boys were home from school to open the photo envelopes. It might've been my imagination, but the kids seemed to have grown taller in the hours we were apart. They hovered over the kitchen table, politely interested on my behalf but not enough to sit down, eager to return to their interior worlds. We flipped through the stack: I got double prints out of decades-old habit, which I sorted into two piles. There were photos of train tracks and the park bench and the creek at odd angles. The AutoZone. One of me that I hadn't noticed them taking, my forehead a knot, staring into space.

Everything's so blurry, my oldest marveled, his frankness not necessarily a complaint.

Where are our friends? asked the younger one. The two boys they had played with were in none of the images. Perhaps my son, used to tapping a phone screen, did not press hard enough on the shutter button. Maybe some of the film had gone bad. We sorted the piles again to be sure. The boys weren't there.

Also missing: the photo I had taken of my own children with their shell collections. The thing is, I knew how to use that camera. I had pressed the button in order to capture them, and somehow had made my children disappear. *Click.*

Now, what were their names, my older son mused, and I wondered if he was being coy. He had an excellent memory. He put index finger to temple, thinking. I had forgotten their names, too, but I could find the father's post if I wanted to. I could use Frank's tablet to relearn the details. I didn't want to. I'd successfully blocked the father via Frank's account and had stayed off his tablet. Would Frank be able to see any of my actions? I had lost track of all the things my husband and I had to discuss. Just because we needed to talk didn't mean we would.

I don't know, I told my children. It was the easiest and worst answer. It was the truth.

In Search Of

His cubicle shuddered for the third time in the last hour, and he automatically began fishing fallen thumbtacks and papers from the crevice where the wall met his desk. He had tried talking to her. He had tried making a joke of it. But no matter what he said, Patricia Trumble's enthusiasm, speed, and girth propelled her rolling desk chair into their shared wall space repeatedly each day.

"Oh my God," she said this time, to no one in particular. "I just took another dominatrix call. What is it about Wednesdays? Tie me up, down, all around. Whew! It's really more a Friday kind of call. People getting freaky in the middle of the week now. Or maybe they're better planners, looking for weekend dates."

He tried tuning her out, his last best coping mechanism.

The two of them were among five advertising account managers for the city's entertainment and political newsweekly, where they shared a small section of the office away from those who dealt with business accounts. They took dictation for paid personal ads they would type, format, and ship to the layout department.

"I mean, would you place an ad like that?" she asked. "Or maybe I should ask, would you respond to an ad like that?"

He kept his head down, focused on his computer screen, so Patricia stood to see him over the cubicle wall. She waved that week's thick broadsheet like a flag she had set on fire. "Yoo-hoo! Earth to Paul, come in Paul. Mr. Cake, Patricia's on line one."

Patricia, a woman of indeterminate age, gazed at him with clear-blue eyes. Her teeth were straight and pearly. Paul would not call her fat; he knew that was unkind. He had described his coworker to his girlfriend as big-boned, heavyset, plus-size. On the larger side. She got winded walking up the three flights to the office. Paul grew uncomfortable when they both walked in together from the parking lot. Her huffing made him antsy, as did her attention, which seemed to be a cross between flirting and bullying. Sheila laughed at his descriptions, which had become a bit between them.

"I didn't hear you," he said to Patricia. "I was busy. Working." He had been staring at his *Far Side* calendar, calculating the time until he would earn his two-week vacation. Ten more months and well into 2004, a whole new year of his life taken up by this work. If he lasted that long at the paper.

"Yeah, right. Your phone hasn't rung in twenty minutes. You didn't hit 'silent,' did you?"

The 'silent' feature, which transferred all his calls to Patricia's line, was switched on. He punched it off. "No," he lied.

"Oh. Well, this woman was inquiring as to how much information should she include, like whips, or just the leather."

His phone rang and he arranged his headset, shutting Patricia out. He would sometimes leave work and notice his reflection in car windows, his gelled hair scrunched down by the black plastic headband that connected to the mouthpiece.

Patricia loomed over his shoulder as he clicked in the boxes on the computer screen. The box marked "Single White Female" created "SWF," and many a client had tittered, "Just like the movie." The computer formatted the page layout. It was a pretty easy job, aside from being suffocated by Patricia's overbearing presence. He had wanted a job at the city's daily newspaper, but the editors told him he needed actual experience. In the two years since earning a master's degree in journalism, this was the closest he had come. Previously, his collection of post-college jobs included car salesman, Abercrombie & Fitch employee, and temp-for-hire.

His and Patricia's cubicles emanated constant chatter, keyboard clacking, a mostly businesslike demeanor mixed with an occasional neutral joke. (They used caution in joking with the lonely-hearted—their sensitivities colored everything. "They put the 'personal' in Personals!" editor-in-chief Bix Crawford would say, often enough to be grating.) After hanging up, especially if the boss was out, Patricia liked to give loud, opinionated commentary that the rest of the department ignored. Paul, her nearest coworker, could only ignore so much.

"Anything good?" Patricia asked him before he even placed the receiver back in its cradle. "Come on, was it a sexy one?"

He thought of a few dirty, inappropriate responses. He already knew he would tell Sheila about this conversation. But now he held back.

"Standard," he said. "The usual."

She peered at the screen over his shoulder. "Does that say dog? It says dog! SWF seeks SWM with dog! Sweet Jesus. So that's your idea of standard? Standard poodle, maybe. What do they do with the dog? Let him up on the bed? I bet collars are involved."

"Maybe she just wants someone to go to the park with," he said. "Maybe she just likes dogs."

"A little touchy about the dogs, are we? Sorry I asked." She went back to her cubicle, muttering her usual refrain: "Oh, the sad, sad people out there. What happened in your childhood, sweetie?"

He didn't know who she meant this time: him, or the SWF seeking man with dog.

Once Patricia left for lunch, he called Sheila at work. Patricia usually got takeout from Shanghai Delight. She would bring back multiple grease-soaked brown paper sacks carrying sticky spareribs, large Styrofoam bins containing fried rice and crunchy noodles, and a small vat of sugared soda. Her keyboard suffered. Fingertips coated in grease and sauces handled the keys, and letters or periods or the spacebar would get stuck in place. Roger, the company tech expert, semiannually visited Patricia's cubicle with an extra keyboard tucked under his arm. When he left, he invariably muttered, "Use a napkin for God's sake. A wet-nap. They're free."

Patricia was unbothered, keeping her top drawer filled with the unused, square, moist towelettes from the Chinese takeout. Saving them, Paul supposed, for some bigger mess. He waited for Sheila to answer the phone at the insurance agency for their daily conversation, which always involved Patricia stories, gossip Sheila reveled in since their awkward first meeting six months ago.

They were at a company party, shortly after Paul started the job. Sheila, hardly one for tact, had asked Patricia when she was due. Patricia set her cocktail on an end table in Bix Crawford's ultra-modern living room, patted the rolls of her unpregnant belly, and confided, "Well first of all, sweetie, I've got to get myself *laid*. That usually comes before getting knocked up, if I'm not mistaken. I think I still remember how it's done. Know anybody who can handle the likes of me?" She eyed Paul across the room, nudging Sheila painfully in the arm with her surprisingly bony elbow. "What, I bet he's wild, huh? He likes to get all the pervert calls. A dirty boy, that one. Am I right or am I right?"

Sheila, speechless, had rejoined Paul across the room to tattle. Patricia waggled her fingers at them. He had been mock-mortified for Sheila's sake, and privately pleased for his own: his girlfriend of one year had been in the wrong, his coworker handled it hilariously, and to top it all off, she had imagined him more sexily than he imagined himself.

Sheila answered on the fifth ring. A routine dieter, Sheila denied herself carbs and fed on daily Patricia stories. Now he regaled Sheila with the latest installment: the bear-in-a-forest noise with which she devoured a bag of microwave popcorn that morning. Eating habits and sex talk were the hallmarks of these tales. Paul would never admit it, but the details stirred him.

"She's a fiend," he told Sheila. "I think she's about five minutes away from jumping me."

He heard a rustle, and flushed apple-red when he realized the noise came from Patricia's desk. She was never quiet. She had managed to surprise him.

"Yeah, yeah, the customers," he said, in no way covering his mistake. "They're pretty crazy. Well, I've got calls coming in."

The phones sounded all afternoon, as if those seeking dates were duty-bound to find them. In the occasional lull, it was totally silent. Patricia still hadn't spoken to him by the time Bix Crawford came by their pod late in the afternoon. He pinned a flyer to the outside of the cubicle wall, updating "Your Rights as an Employee," a tiny-print poster that the company lawyers provided.

"Kids, how's business?" Bix asked them. He rarely waited for replies. "Patty, listen, we're having an editor's meeting, and I want you to sit in. Paul can handle the phones. It's about one of the ads you took—the guy who goes by 'White Male.' Just White Male, no single, no searching. People are calling left and right. This guy has become an instant celebrity. He's loved and hated."

Patricia stood up, blushing. "I get so many calls. But his. Yeah, it stood out a little."

Paul snatched last week's paper from the stand and opened to the personals. There he was, just as Bix said:

WHITE MALE
STOP BLAMING IT ALL ON ME.
NOT EVERYTHING'S MY FAULT.
I'VE GOT MY OWN PROBLEMS.
GET OVER IT.

The advertising department wanted to run the ads on the side panels of buses, on park benches, anywhere the newsweekly's name could be attached. Bix said they had to set up a second voice mailbox to accept all the calls White Male was receiving. Other calls to the main switchboard both praised and criticized White Male—and the paper. Some saw the ad as political, racist, a joke.

"It's a freedom-of-speech issue," Bix, a white male, said. "Self-expression, and it's about time somebody said it. Way to land a real moneymaker, Patty!"

Paul sloppily folded the paper and stalked off.

In his kitchen that night, he popped open two bottles of imported Belgian ale, handing one to Sheila. He took a long swig before launching into his regular tirade about the day's events. He was sure that Patricia had overheard his insults, and his guilt felt thick on his tongue. Then he felt angry at Patricia for making him feel guilty.

"She's like this hippo, right?" Paul demonstrated his coworker's walk. "But she's a hippo on too much caffeine. A really loud, obnoxious hippo. Or maybe she's a drunk hippo. It's all like 'Bang! Whap! Fer Chrissakes!' Knocking over the cubicle, trampling small children. Every move she makes is an event."

Sheila giggled, egging him on. He was beginning to feel worse. He drank from his beer and looked through the cupboard for something to eat. Sheila shrugged off her tailored black suit jacket and sipped the beer, smearing lipstick on the bottle.

"Order a pizza?" he asked.

"You know I'm on Atkins. Get me a salad, please." Sheila already was as thin as a catalog model, but she insisted she needed to lose more weight. She claimed her hair and even her eyes shone brightly when she hit her target weight, which was ten pounds lighter than the recommendation for a five-foot-five woman. He had looked it up once, concerned.

She handed him the phone. "Hurry, Patricia's probably about to tie up their line with her order."

He dialed, facing the shiny black door of the microwave, and in its reflection he could see the usual headset indentation in his hair. He smoothed it out with his hand, feeling the stiffness of dried hair gel. Sheila often told him his hair looked good and she liked how it smelled, but she never touched it.

Since the age of fifteen, he had always had girlfriends, women who fit easily beneath one arm. He was strong but not threatening, good-looking in a forgettable way. Even when he wore a shirt and tie, well-shined shoes, and expensive khaki pants, it was easy to picture him in his fraternity sweatshirt and dingy white baseball hat, being force-fed beer after beer through a plastic funnel. The *Weekly*'s dress code was nonexistent, a form of self-styled office casual that ranged from coveralls to peppy holiday sweaters, but he insisted on dressing the part for the job he wanted to have—advice from the professor of the one management course he took in college. Still, touches of his fraternity days remained: the tie a bit too jaunty, a shirttail left untucked, a little too much crunch to his gelled hair. Moving between girlfriends, with hardly a pause in between.

He ordered a large pepperoni pizza, plus a Greek salad for Sheila. They ate in front of the television, watching three half-hour situation comedies before going into the bedroom. They had sex, and much as he tried to dismiss the day's events, his mind kept going back to Patricia.

"Nice," Sheila sighed when he rolled off of her. She usually fell asleep immediately after.

"Yeah," he said.

"You OK?" she asked.

He thought for a moment. "Oh, it's just work stuff. There's this personals guy calling himself 'White Male.' They're all hopped up about it, Patricia and Bix. All she did was answer the phone."

"So, you wished you'd answered the phone instead?" Sheila asked, her eyes already closed.

"I guess," he said.

"Then all you would've done is answer the phone, too," she said.

"That's not the point," he said, but she didn't answer. By her breathing he could tell she was asleep.

Paul stared at the ceiling. Sheila snored lightly next to him. He rolled on his side and looked at her for a while, trying to discern her features in the dark. Her face held aspects of other girls he had dated: Bridget's upturned nose, Amber's freckles, Layla's long eyelashes. Or was it Amber's nose, and Bridget's freckles? He couldn't remember. He slept without dreaming.

The next day was relatively quiet until Patricia's friend Peggy called. When Patricia talked to Peggy on the phone, she seemed to be engaged in a game of high-stakes charades, but with shrieking laughter. Paul was having trouble hearing the callers on his line. He had already been slapped on the wrist a month ago by Bix after he accidentally placed two hetero ads in the "Bi-Curious" section, and he was sure Patricia's distractions caused his mistake . Bix had connections at the daily paper and kept promising to introduce Paul to the city desk editors there. Paul first had to improve, maybe move up to reporter, before he would get noticed. With the latest White Male business—he now was placing an ad, sometimes two, every week—Patricia was upstaging him. Patricia had worked at the weekly almost a decade, since graduating from the City Business College, and had no aspirations to work elsewhere.

Patricia's extended conversation forced the glut of all incoming calls to his phone. He waved at her quickly, a little too subtle for her to see. He laid a hand on Patricia's padded shoulder, cringing with the immediate reaction he knew it would provoke.

"AAAAAGUPPTH!" she shouted in her friend's ear. "Holy Christ, Paul. You scared me shitless. You shouldn't sneak up on people like that." She turned her back to him again.

"Peg, I gotta go. I'll call you later. Yeah, no freakin' shit."

She expertly knocked the phone back into its cradle and whipped off her headset, tearing a few bleach-blond hairs with it.

"This had better be good, Paul Cake."

He must've flinched, because Patricia turned sweet. She batted her eyelashes and flashed a pretty smile.

"Cake, sweetie, I'm only messing with ya. Relax. What can Miss Patricia do for you?"

He spoke fast, anticipating the inevitable ring of the phone.

"It's not that big a deal. It's just that, when you're talking, you know, on the phone, I can't, I have a hard time."

The phone rang, and in one fluid motion, she swiveled in her chair, realigned her headset atop her teased hairdo, and lifted the receiver.

"Personals, this is Patricia. How may I help you?"

She waved him off and began to type the new ad. He looked briefly at her screen. "SWM in search of S&M. Amazons, big biceps, thighs like vise."

"Just your type," Paul muttered, walking back to his desk.

Patricia talked to White Male once every couple days, and Paul suspected he was calling other times, too; there were more hang-ups, probably because White Male was trying for Patricia's line. He knew when Patricia got a call from him. Her tone would become breathier. She never discussed the calls after hanging up, the way she would with the others. Paul would check the computer system to see the latest ads before they ran in the paper:

WHITE MALE
YOU'LL BE WORKING
FOR ME SOMEDAY.
WHY NOT START NOW?

and

WHITE MALE
I CAN'T GET HIRED,
BUT I'M NOT BLAMING ANYONE.
DATE ME.

It was all a bit much. Paul was a white male, too, but he had nothing to prove. In Paul's opinion, this guy was asking for trouble. Paul didn't see a reason to make a stir. White Male was making a stir.

A few weeks later, Patricia took a call, and Paul immediately knew it was the guy. Against policy, he pressed "silent" on his phone and ignored the incoming calls.

"I like your voice, too," she was saying, "Listen, I know you're white and I know you're male. What about single?"

Paul involuntarily flexed his quadriceps and pushed his chair into the wall of his cubicle. Patricia was purring in such a low voice, Paul had to hold his breath to hear.

"Why don't we cut out the middleman?" she was saying.

He needed to walk. He strode the hallway to the vending machines, feigning great interest in the dusty packets of peanuts and Zagnut bars. He examined the empty slots, imagining Patricia holding an open bag beneath the catch-tray like a lottery winner. In reality, she hadn't been frequenting the vending machines like she used to. In fact, in the last month, she seemed somehow different. Paul suddenly knew what was missing: a good twenty pounds. He wondered if she was dieting and losing weight because of his careless comments. Or because of White Male. Why now, he thought, and why did he even care?

He walked back to his desk, and purposely passed Patricia's cubicle instead of going around the long way. She was running her fingers through her headset-tousled hair. She had had it cut a new way, and strands framed her face in soft wisps. Paul felt a strange pang for his coworker, which he usually defined as pity. This time, it was different.

Patricia turned and caught Paul staring. She gave him a sly grin.

"Take a picture, Cake, it'll last longer." She flipped her hair and swiveled back to her computer monitor. "Is your phone on 'silent'? I'm getting a metric shit ton of calls."

"Yeah, sorry. I had to take a quick break."

He punched the button and immediately the phone started ringing. Patricia's phone was ringing, too.

"Patricia?"

Her hand paused over the receiver, her headset already back in place.

"Your hair looks nice."

Patricia smiled and shook her head, as if to scold him. But things were thawing, he could tell. He sat down and picked up his phone, trying to ignore the blush creeping up his neck and cheeks. "Personals, this is Paul. Can I help you?"

At the end of their shift, they walked out together. Usually Paul waited for Patricia to leave first. But he found himself wanting to talk to her.

She spoke first. "Paul, I need a favor. It's kind of a big one."

He was taken aback, immediately thinking up excuses, but she didn't give him a chance to speak.

"Listen, I figure you owe me," she said. "You know, after what you said on the phone that day."

"When?" he feigned confusion. "What day? I'd be happy to help if I can."

She seemed to accept his lie, and he was pleased to be back in her good graces.

"It's classified info. Not like the classifieds. Like, a don't-you-dare-fucking-tell-anyone favor. Can I trust you?"

"Of course."

She drew a deep breath as they reached their cars. Patricia's new Volkswagen Jetta and Paul's old Buick Regal were parked nose-to-nose in the small lot.

"OK, look, I don't know what the company policy is as far as getting involved," she began, and Paul felt his heart involuntarily jump. "But I've been talking to one of the callers, a regular. He does an ad every week, pretty much. You probably know who I'm talking about, since we practically sit on top of each other."

White Male, Paul thought with venom. He nodded mutely.

"It's White Male," she said. "We decided it's time we meet face-to-face. In ten years here, I swear, I've never come close to doing this. I'm kind of freaked out about going by myself, to be honest. What if the guy's a psychopath? That would be just my luck with men, not that you care. Not that you need to know. I asked my girlfriend Peggy, but she has to work. I'd kind of feel better anyway if it was a guy who went with."

Paul interrupted Patricia's babbling. "Sure, OK, yeah. When?"

She sighed. "I know it's short notice, but I told him I'd go tonight."

Paul had planned to have dinner at Sheila's.

"No problem," he told Patricia.

She gave him directions to the coffee shop, and he called Sheila on his cell phone from the car. He couldn't tell her the truth, not after his relentless mocking of Patricia over the last six months.

"I don't think I'm coming over tonight," he told her. "I'm really tired."

"Come on, I wanted to make the Chilean sea bass," Sheila said. "I can't eat it all by myself. I'll give you a back rub."

"Sorry. I might be coming down with something. Don't want you to get sick."

He punched the cell phone's hang-up button. Instead of feeling guilty for lying, he felt free. He pulled his car in behind Patricia's on the street in front of the coffee shop. A nice, neutral meeting point. It was 6:30 p.m. They were a half hour early.

On the way in, Paul tripped over nothing on the sidewalk, and Patricia laughed as if it were a pratfall, as if he had done it for her amusement. They didn't know how to act outside of the office. There was a brief tussle over who would open the door, and Patricia strong-armed it while he stood aside dumbly.

"Sit near me, but don't sit with me," she stage-whispered, with all the subtlety of a young child telling a secret. He noticed she was wearing a blouse he had never seen before. It was red and shiny, like a present. Her hair had new highlights. They wound up at two tables for two, pushed flush against a wall with a mural depicting the street outside. Neither ordered anything from the counter, where a twentysomething girl in a formfitting shirt and baggy blue jeans wiped down the day's coffee spills. She gave Paul an easy smile. Paul faced the counter, and Patricia faced the storefront window with the view of the bar across the street. They sat back-to-back.

"So, what now?" Paul asked.

"Now we wait. Read the paper or something. You don't have to do anything, just be backup. Turn around! I don't want him to know I have backup."

At quarter to seven, Patricia's cell phone rang. "Hi, Mom," she said. "No, I'm here but I'm waiting. Because I'm early, that's why. Listen, is everything OK? Are you all right? Then I'm going to call you later. I can't talk now. Yes, that's what I said." She hung up.

Paul couldn't resist a jab. "Does your mother approve of your fraternizing with strange men in coffee shops?"

"Paul, really, you're not so strange," she said, her voice low and flirtatious. She laughed. "Mom's all for it. It's hard to meet people anymore, and I'm not getting any younger."

"C'mon, you're not old. You're what, forty, forty-two tops?"

"Thirty-eight." She didn't sound offended, just resigned. "And how old are you, Mr. Cake?"

"Twenty-seven."

They were quiet. Paul's digital watch beeped at the hour.

"My watch is fast," Paul lied.

Patricia sighed. "Thanks."

"What about you, still seeing that same girl?" she asked.

"Sheila? Yeah, we still see each other. It's not serious, though." As soon as the words were out of his mouth, he knew they were true. He also knew that Sheila would not characterize their relationship that way.

"Then what's the point?" Patricia said. "If it's not serious. I mean, sex, yeah, sure. But what about the rest of it? Don't you want something more substantial?"

"Um, hold on, you don't know me or her at all," Paul said. "Don't you think you're making some assumptions here?"

"But am I right?"

Sheila's attractiveness was what drew him to her, and the sex was good if not great. He instinctively knew their relationship was "for now," which made it manageable, easy. Though lately they had less and less to talk about, and couldn't even agree on what to have for dinner.

"Never mind," she said. "Your silence says it all."

"Oh, sure, you take personal ads for a living, suddenly you're a psychologist?" He stood up to leave. "I don't know why I came."

"No? I do. Because you felt guilty. Because you owed me. Sounds like you owe your girlfriend more than you've given her, too."

He swiveled to face her. "Mind your own fucking business, Patricia. Did you make all this up, to get me here? Is there actually a White Male? I bet it's you. What, do you want to date me?"

Patricia narrowed her eyes, calculating, and the vulnerability of a moment ago vanished. "Is that what you think?" she asked. "That I'd ask you out by tricking you into coming here? Because that must be the only way I can get a date, huh?"

"That wasn't what I meant," he said, confused by how quickly she had turned the tables. He hadn't meant to imply those things. He was half-expecting her to say Exactly, yes, I want to date you. He wanted her to say it.

She was looking past him now. "You should go," she said.

"No, I'm your backup," he said. "I'll see this through."

"I changed my mind," she said. "He's here. He doesn't look like a serial killer. Please go. Please?"

White Male, a plain but not unattractive thirtysomething with dark hair, walked in with the weekly under his arm. His smile turned into a huge grin as he spotted Patricia at the table. He held out the newspaper like he was being carded for ID at a bar.

"Patricia?" he asked. "I'm, well, you know who I am." Patricia beamed as they shook hands, holding on a beat too long.

"Great to meet you," she said, more shy than he had ever seen her.

"Were my ads too much?" White Male asked her. "The letters to the editor kind of blew my mind. I never thought—"

"Oh, not at *all*," she said.

Paul slunk away to the other side of the coffee shop. He didn't want to hear Patricia reassure this guy. It was too late to drink coffee, he thought, as White Male ordered at the counter.

"I hope you got decaf," Paul hissed to Patricia, furious with his ineptitude. She shooed him outside with a flick of a wrist, mouthing the word,

"Go!" He was glad to take his reddened face outside to cool off. Through the plate glass, Patricia was watching him. Was she having second thoughts? Then she rubbed her nose with her middle finger. Flipping Paul the bird.

White Male casually returned to the table with a tray of coffee and cake slices. Paul read Patricia's lips: "My favorite!"

He watched. The two sat across from each other with sickeningly eager smiles on their faces, their flirtatiousness an affront. Paul felt like he had at fifteen, relegated to the kids' table at Christmas dinner while his older cousins got raucous in the kitchen over beers and boxed wine. Fine. Good for Patricia, then. He did and didn't mean it, ambivalence leaving him lightheaded. The feeling would compel him to stay home from work the next day, redialing the weekly paper through the main switchboard and asking for his own department. Each time he heard Patricia's voice on the line, he came closer to making a decision besides hanging up.

White Hands

Joanne was on the way to collect her children from piano lessons when the car's engine light came on. She had left work a half hour early, speeding, her thoughts fluttering around but never landing, and she only noticed the red dashboard light when she tried to accelerate and the Civic slowed to a crawl. She pulled over to the side of the road, where the car sputtered and died. The nearest service station was miles away, but plenty of daylight shone on the corn and wheat fields surrounding the two-lane highway, and she had a cell phone. She called the towing company first, then her husband, Todd, who was an apprentice to an insurance broker. He often worked unpaid overtime; the car trouble meant he would have to leave work early to pick up the kids. His boss watched him closely, marking his comings and goings. Joanne could hear Todd's sigh over the phone, a sigh she understood and tried not to take personally.

Still. She couldn't help but feel pleased, like a kid ditching school must, as she sat in her car waiting for the tow truck, rocked by the occasional sudden breeze of passing tractor trailers on the two-lane highway. The car was a pain, and probably would be an expensive pain, but the breakdown afforded her an afternoon free pass. For lack of anything better to do, she examined herself in the rearview mirror. Her hair had started to come undone from the twist she had created that morning, but her makeup was intact. Her light wool work suit, the gray, was a little wrinkled, but could go another wearing before it needed to be dry cleaned. Not long after she had readjusted the mirror, the truck appeared in it, with the company logo, "Earl's Towing," painted backwards so it could be read in a reflection. The driver's blond hair flopped from the air whooshing through both open windows. He appeared to be singing, or shouting to himself.

He was a youngish man, maybe late twenties or early thirties. He clambered out of the truck and towards her car, leaning down into her open window. His shirt bore a red-and-white oval patch, with "Earl" stitched in red script. Joanne held out her soft, thin hand and introduced herself.

"Earl," she said, "thank you so much for coming to pick me up. I hope it wasn't any trouble."

Her tone made clear it did not matter if it was any trouble. She was a paying customer conducting a business transaction. She mentally noted to double-check that the credit card had room for the charge. She might have to juggle some expenses, like the latest payment for piano lessons. Her tone of voice was culled from years as a temp agency's office manager, a job she had managed to keep even though organization was not her strong suit.

"You think I'm Earl?" the man asked. "Jeez, that's funny. Oh, man. Big Earl's gonna love this."

He had a youthful face, still tanned from the summer, and shaggy blond hair. Something about his nose seemed strange. Joanne decided it would fit better on an older man's face. She admitted to herself that he didn't look like an Earl, a name she tagged to a gentleman with a serious demeanor.

"Your shirt says Earl," she pointed out.

The man looked down at his shirt as if he were surprised to see it, surprised to find himself wearing a shirt at all. He looked up at Joanne with eyes as blue and piercing as a Siberian husky.

"So it does," he said. "But I'm Brian."

He finally shook her hand and indicated with a wave that she should climb in.

The tow truck's front seat and floor were littered with crinkled fast-food wrappers, spent cigarette packs, and enough dried mud to assemble a model volcano for a grade-school science project.

Joanne eyed the passenger-side floorboards, trying to decide where to place her leather pumps without damaging them. She started to raise one foot into the cab, which made her skirt ride up. She looked like a caricature of a businesswoman and she knew this. On the other side of the vehicle, through the open driver's side door, Brian glanced leisurely at her legs and then away. He spat on the ground, delicately.

"Don't be shy, now," he said. "Just hike 'er up."

After a moment's hesitation, she turned to sit in the passenger seat, swinging her legs into the cab. There was no avoiding the mess on the floor, so her shoes landed atop a Styrofoam cup and a brown paper sack that jangled and crunched like broken glass.

"Attagirl," the man said. "Careful with your feet, there. Bag's full of broken glass."

She didn't ask why, only murmured her thanks.

After he had hooked up her dead car, he started the truck and signaled to merge onto the highway. When he shifted gears, he looked like a twelve-year-old boy at the controls of a video game.

"Sheesh," he chuckled. "Earl."

On the phone, Todd had sighed like wind whistling through an empty canyon. By the week, her husband's exasperation with her seemed to grow. Unloading groceries in disbelief: You didn't get chunky peanut butter? Followed by a long exhalation that seemed designed to calm him. Today on the phone he had wondered when she last had the car serviced. He said, You've got to get your head out of the clouds, Joanne.

He was being unfair; she couldn't help the car breaking down. But last week, she could've helped. She had called Todd to ask him to pick up the kids at the YMCA, where Jenna took gymnastics and Robbie played Ping-Pong (incessantly, methodically.) She had no plans. She just knew she didn't feel like picking up the kids. She didn't want to abandon them—nothing like that. She just wanted someone else to deal with them.

On the phone, Todd had tried to tease her.

"Going to meet your boyfriend?" he asked.

She could've told him she was going to the mall, or she could've invented a doctor's appointment. Instead she was vague.

"I just need a break is all," she said. "I've got some things I want to take care of before dinner."

"Sort of a get-your-shit-together-without-the-kids-in-your-hair thing?"

She paused. "Right. Sure."

His voice aimed for cheery but came out flat. "Well, get it together."

She tried not to let him ruin her afternoon. She walked around a small strip of stores, browsing shop windows, imagining herself in other clothing: teenager jeans and batik tank tops. She even tried on a blouse, disappointed that it made her look frowsy, pregnant. She wasn't pregnant. She didn't consider herself a frump. She passed a salon and considered coloring her hair. Some of the younger girls who came into the temp agency had bright blond highlights. They wore tight sweaters, pencil skirts, shiny boots that climbed up firm calves. They carried an air that yes, this would be temporary work until something much grander, more important and worldly, came along. Joanne, accurately or not, sensed their scorn. As if her managerial position was the same as replacing a secretary out for a C-section, an assignment that might last six weeks. At most.

She passed the salon, ducking into the small bookstore with the hardwoods and floor-to-ceiling shelves. She had never been much of a reader but she found herself content with browsing, becoming immersed in a pulp novel about vampires who fall in love with average humans. When a clerk came down the aisle, she felt herself shift to hide the book cover, embarrassment creeping up her spine with a tingle. She didn't know where the feeling came from. But there it was.

That morning, after arriving at her small office in her then-functioning Civic, Joanne had remained in the car to fix her hair and face. She never did it at home. It seemed a vanity, a luxury, to linger at the sink in the bathroom. Todd needed to shave and the children needed to brush their teeth and wet down their straw-like hair after a night's sleep. The house had a single bathroom with a stand-up shower. She dreamed about bathtubs the way some women dreamed of men.

She had been married eight years, and with each day she grew more remote from her single self, the one who wore low-cut shirts of silky material, who thought nothing of dropping fifty bucks on drinks in a single evening. Ten more she fed to the jukebox so she could dance, whether or not somebody joined her on the scuffed dance floor. Used to be she would charge hundreds at a department store makeup counter. At home in her efficiency, she would spend an hour on her eyes alone. Impractical, and she had not been particularly happy or satisfied with that life, yet she tied those years to a nostalgia that bordered on reverence.

It wasn't that she let herself go after marriage. No. She could still turn heads, in the right type of clothes, or if she spent time on her hair. What she had let go of was an idea of herself. Every morning in her office parking lot, she tried, with varying results, to remember that idea, if only to last through the day. Her routine was to arrive a few minutes early and pull down the visor mirror, pushing her brown hair around until it was a style. She would apply bright lipstick.

Today when she had gotten out of the car, she straightened her skirt and looked at her reflection in the window of the sandwich shop next door to the office. It took a moment for her image to give way to the employee standing behind it, a boy of about eighteen or nineteen, washing the inside of the glass storefront window. He smiled, then pursed his lips into a whistle. Unobserved by the people she lived with, but watched and appreciated by the sandwich maker. A flush spread in her cheeks, and she found herself smiling into the window, at both her reflection and what was behind it.

B rian-not-Earl drove the tow truck at a moderate speed along the highway. He frequently glanced in the rearview, checking the cargo, but largely disregarded his passenger. The radio, tuned to the classical station, spat out crackly Vivaldi.

"'The Four Seasons,' I think," Joanne said. "This is 'Fall.'"

"Huh?" He seemed surprised, despite the fact he had picked her up, by her presence in his truck.

She tried again. "Do you like classical music?"

"Sure I do," he said. "Very much so."

They traveled at least a mile in silence, Joanne watching the brownish cornfields as if looking for a message. She commuted forty minutes each way, every day, and the drive was manageable save for reasons such as these: emergency, inconvenience, the awkward conversation—or lack thereof—between strangers. Out the window, a windmill she had never noticed before glinted and turned lazily in the sun. They were nearing Sheridan, the first of four small towns en route to Joanne's mechanic.

"I've got to make a pit stop," Brian announced. He pulled into the parking lot of a roadhouse that advertised draft beer with neon signs, but didn't appear to have a name of its own. There were two other cars in the lot, one parked in front of a placard that read "Employee of the Month Parking ONLY."

"Just a quick errand," he said. "I'll be right back."

Todd also said he had to make a pit stop when he went to the bathroom. Joanne looked at her watch. She would've tapped her toe, a habit of hers, if the cab's floor didn't present a safety hazard.

"I need to get home relatively soon," she said.

"I'll be quick as a flash. You can come in if you want."

She shook her head no, a reflex. He ambled into the bar, not at all quick as a flash, but like a man tired from a long day, a long career. In need of refreshment for his thirst and his life. He was probably thirty, just a few years younger than Joanne. He carried the spacey, harmless affectation of his generation, of men who had not yet grown up.

His jeans were clean and dark blue, and he wore thick-soled work boots that seemed to slow him down even more. His collared "Earl" shirt hung untucked around his waist, though it was still easy to see he was fit in the way people who perform manual labor are fit, and in the way those who sit at a desk are not. Joanne spent much of her day on the phone, at the computer, in meetings. She had always been thin, but after having the kids, she noticed a softening and rounding, as if her body had gone slack. Certainly her sedentary job contributed. At least, she consoled herself, she had her own office.

She sat patiently for exactly seven and a half minutes, then began to shift in her seat, aiming for a more comfortable position that didn't involve disturbing the glass and wrappers. She failed. She checked the time repeatedly, noting the probable progression of her family's life with each tick of her silver Timex: Now Robbie is complaining to Mrs. Printz that his fingers hurt, and he wants to stop practicing. Now Jenna shushes her younger brother, but looks at the clock to gauge how much time is left. Now Mrs. Printz, the retired elementary school music teacher, notices Jenna's glance (and probably her dirty fingernails) and remarks, "Well, we needn't worry about the time, children. Your mother doesn't, after all." Now Todd arrives on the dot, smoothing over everything and surprising the kids. Perhaps with a wink for Mrs. Printz. Todd was a winker. He had winked at Joanne the night they met, at an automotive parts store's Christmas party. Neither had worked at the store. They had come as other people's dates.

Ten minutes passed. Joanne rarely went to bars anymore. She spent a good deal of time in them during her early twenties, before meeting Todd, and she associated them with groping and woozy intimations and things better left unsaid that got said anyway, after a few drinks. She once told a very nice bartender she was sure he could get a real job if he only tried, and another time told a man she had just met that his hands looked like they knew how to touch a woman. Regret: a welling in the throat with the remnants of words that should have been choked down. She had stood on tables, exposed her shiny nylon underwear, pulled up her shirt, danced so close to both men and women that she knew the fit of these strangers' bodies through a layer of denim.

It made her cringe, nearly ten years later, despite the relative comfort of her life—the A-frame house, the weekly taco night and meals she could make blindfolded, her children snug in twin beds that she had purchased for half off, dreaming their inexplicable worlds, and Todd, who was fine, who was Todd. Those comforts provided the general assurance that she was done, and she would not have to put herself out there like that again. The thing of it was, she still liked bars. Maybe just the thought of bars. The smoke and the nicked wooden tables and the taste of something cold and bitter on her tongue. Excitement, possibility, in the form of a free evening. Todd rarely drank, and cigarette smoke bothered him. She used to be a smoker but quit when they were dating. Which was fortunate. Less than a year after she met Todd, before they had even discussed marriage, she became pregnant with Jenna.

She checked her watch again, and seven more minutes had passed. It was getting chillier, and she shivered slightly. When was the last time she had been to a bar? When was the last time she'd had a beer, for that matter? Joanne couldn't recall. Maybe at her cousin's wedding. That was several months ago, in the summer. She considered going inside, under the pretense of retrieving Brian. What she really wanted was to have a drink. She would walk in—given the number of cars in the lot, he would be easy to find—and tell him that as long as he was finishing his drink, she might as well have one, too.

Todd wouldn't get it. Why hadn't she just called home, why hadn't she just stayed in the truck? Todd dealt with insurance: he knew the risks of any possible endeavor. He would expect her to stay in the truck. Brian had asked her to come in, but probably guessed she would refuse. And she did.

What else was to be expected of her, in that light wool suit and pumps? Once she had worn designer jeans that cost as much as having a car towed. Heels so high she would twist an ankle stumbling from a bar in the hours that were too late for day, too early for night.

She wished she were wearing a different shirt, even one that made her look frowsy and like she was trying too hard. Anything but this suit. She smudged on lipstick without looking in a mirror. Her hand was on the metal door handle, ready to yank it, when Brian swung out the bar's wooden door and crunched through the gravel. His collar was somewhat askew, as if he had taken off his shirt and put it back on again without bothering to unbutton it. He brought a smoky smell into the truck, plus a brown paper sack that he placed on the floor near the others at her feet. He looked at Joanne, his eyes slightly bloodshot. He smiled, and Joanne thought she could smell beer on his breath.

"Thank you for your patience," he said to her. "We at Earl's Towing appreciate it."

Joanne still wanted that drink. Had decided on it.

"Hope you didn't rush on my account," she said. She grinned, then wondered if she had lipstick on her teeth and pursed her lips instead.

His Siberian husky eyes looked at her, quizzical. His nose, she saw up close, was crooked and reddened.

"Because we could go back in, if you didn't have time to finish your drink, that is," she said. Her voice slipped around the sentence, the words sloshing in her mouth.

"What, you want to go in now?" Brian asked.

Joanne thought it was an invitation. "Sure. Yes."

He started the truck and gripped the gear shift knob. The motor hummed. "But why?" he asked. He sounded like one of her children.

Joanne's brow wrinkled. She pushed her bangs off her forehead, and suddenly wished she were talking to Todd, with all his answers anticipated and prepared for. A man expert in percentages, risk factors, fatalities, causalities. A man who never made her guess. Brian had not yet begun backing up the truck; he waited for Joanne's answer as if her words would shift them into gear or kill the engine.

"I didn't think I wanted to, before," she began. "That was before. Then I thought about it, and I said, 'Why not?'"

She attempted to laugh in a lighthearted fashion. She sounded like a cat whose tail had been shut in a door. Brian considered this for a moment, then checked his mirrors and began reversing. "Why not, why not," he said, parrotlike. "Let's get this show on the road. You probably wouldn't like that place, anyway."

"That's fine," Joanne said, saving face. "Either way is perfectly fine with me."

He snorted. "Tell me this. Do you ever make up your mind one way or the other? And then stick to it? It's not so hard. You should try it sometime."

Joanne's mouth opened and closed noiselessly, a guppy out of water. He was eyeing her, amused, and she turned straight ahead. She counted the white painted dashes on the road to control her temper. Neither spoke for several miles. Brian's cell phone broke the silence of the cab. It played a tinkling music box melody as its ring, and he whistled the last few bars. His whistle was surprisingly high-pitched, but in tune.

"Yell-o," he said. "Hey. How you doing?"

He raised his eyebrows and looked over at Joanne. The phone was wedged between his chin and shoulder and he drove with both hands on the wheel. The tow truck swerved a little, the Civic in back mimicking with a light fishtail.

"Can't. I've got a passenger. A job, man. Know the meaning of the word?"

Joanne moved her feet, causing the bags of glass to jangle again.

"Careful," Brian mouthed. "Glass."

On the dashboard, a figurine of a hula dancer wiggled and shook with all its might. "Greetings from Maui" was painted in careful script on the base. Its small plastic lei was broken and hung like a streamer down the plastic body. Its grass skirt was made of the green plastic found in Easter baskets.

"How long will it take?" Brian said into the phone.

They stood on the front porch of a country house Joanne had driven by many times. It looked abandoned, but when Brian rang the doorbell they could hear the chimes. Joanne called Todd and told him what to fix the kids for dinner. Robbie might eat macaroni and cheese, but he would definitely eat chicken fingers. Jenna would eat just about anything.

"I'm fine, fine," she told Todd breezily, to stave off his surprising worry. "It's just going to take longer than we thought."

She switched off her phone and dropped it into her purse, which was filled with receipts, papers from the children's school, tissue packets and hand sanitizer, an overstuffed day planner she hadn't looked at in weeks, and thirteen tubes of lipstick.

"You'll be late for dinner," Brian said. A challenge.

She waved her hand to dismiss the idea, a foreign-feeling gesture. "They can make their own," she said, decisive. Brian's comment in the truck still stung. He rang the doorbell a second time. Dusk hung a few feet above their heads, soon to fall.

"What are we doing here?" Joanne asked, when it became apparent no one was coming to the door. Brian's features remained immobile. He answered by rote, the way a waiter in a chain restaurant might recite the specials.

"People sometimes like to give me things," he said. "Things I might be able to use. I come pick the stuff up, take it off their hands."

"Oh," Joanne said. "And what do they get from you?"

He seemed to consider the question, studying her face a long while. Joanne couldn't tell if he was confused, disappointed, or something else.

"Let's try around back," he said. He had a springy gait, a shade away from skipping.

The house was surrounded by cornfields, and Joanne was reminded of her high school days, when kids would trek from the suburbs to an abandoned farmhouse surrounded by crops. An empty place where they would be just off the radar, if they were quiet. Rationed beers and joints were passed around; both were in short supply if older brothers and siblings were not around to procure them. They would sit on the porch or in the clearing, trying to scare themselves with ghost stories—the Noose in the Barn, the House with the Glowing Red Light—or coerce one another into the cornfields. One night, a girl named Jenny Almeter, not so much a friend as an acquaintance, had walked so deep into the field that she couldn't hear the others shouting for her. Or said she couldn't. She was gone at least a half hour, and when she stepped out of the corn into the clearing, still not speaking or answering to the hushed yells of her name, her white hands parted the stalks, coming out first as if they were separate from the rest of her body. She emerged fully, hands attached to arms attached to body, and looked around at the others in the partial moonlight. They were babbling their concern and surprise—even Joanne, who hardly knew the girl. Joanne couldn't stop looking at those white hands. When Jenny Almeter finally spoke, her voice sounded as disembodied as her hands had looked.

"You can't hear a thing for all the rustling," she had said.

Back in high school, Joanne had refused to go inside the abandoned house with the other kids; she stood outside and away from the cornfield. She had heard that belongings remained: a child's doll on the floor and ancient canned goods in the cupboard. That farmhouse had seemed dependable, sturdy, as if it could provide for a family just by remaining upright. The reasons to leave such a place, whatever they were, were beyond the scope of Joanne's high school mind. The reasons for wandering off into the corn, equally mystifying.

The house they stood in now still had inhabitants, ones who had recently cooked something with tomato and beef, and left an open newspaper spread on the kitchen table. Brian had entered by turning the unlocked knob of the back door, guiding Joanne into the kitchen by placing a hand at the small of her back. Her muscles tensed slightly, then relaxed.

"It's fine," he said. "I guess nobody's home. Or she's sleeping."

"Who? Are you going to get us arrested?" Her family was thirty miles away. They could have lived on the moon.

Brian laughed, revealing a few crowns on otherwise white teeth. His eyes were no longer red and he seemed steadier than he had after leaving the bar. "Not hardly. Big Earl asked me to swing by. This is his mom's place."

In the living room, a family portrait sat on a table overrun with lace doilies. No one had bothered to dress up for the studio shot. The men wore T-shirts and jeans, the two women were wearing cutoff shorts.

"Which one's Earl?" Joanne asked. "Oh."

Without help she had located the man called Big Earl, dwarfing the rest of his family in height and weight. He was off the charts.

Brian held a cardboard box with his name black-markered on the side. The fresh marker smell filled up the whole room.

"Done admiring Earl & Co.?" he said. "I've got just one more thing to do."

He hoisted the box to get a better grip. The contents clinked and settled.

"If you don't mind," he added.

She looked him in the eyes.

"I don't mind," she said.

They parked alongside the road in a shallow vehicle turnoff. Brian ran his hands through his hair. He said they would have to walk a bit, but it was worth it. His favorite part of the errands.

"Are you scared of the country?" he asked.

She shook her head. She felt utterly at ease and had no explanation for it.

"Good," he said. "No reason to be. City people sometimes get scared out here, but this is the safest place there is."

Joanne cleared her throat. "What you said earlier, in the car . . ." She had been trying to think of the right response ever since, and phrased her words carefully.

"Just an observation," he said.

"But you don't know about all the decisions I make," she said. "All day at work, then all night at home. Eat your fish sticks and take your baths. Brush your teeth. Remember to write a note, reminding myself to wash the kids' clothes. Do I order yellow legal pads, white legal pads, blue lines, or red lines? It's exhausting."

"But those aren't important decisions, are they?" he asked. "More like directions than decisions."

"They matter to some people."

"Do they matter to you?"

She didn't answer, and Brian was quiet for a moment, too. "Who cares about making a kid take a bath?" he said finally. "So he doesn't take a bath. He'll stink, and the kids at school will make fun of him. Then see who's lining up for the tub at night."

Joanne smiled inwardly, though her face remained impassive. "Let's go already," she said. She was making decisions.

The field was about a half mile from the road, he said. Could she walk in those shoes?

She said she could. He carried the clinking bags of broken glass, and he handed her another bag that held whole bottles.

"Wine?" she asked, though the bag was light. He shook his head and said they were empties.

"Too bad," she said, wondering at herself. He handed her a little silver flask. It was warm from his hip pocket. "It's not wine," he said. She took a sip, choking the liquor down. He was humming the music they had heard earlier on the radio.

"The Vivaldi?" he said. "That was 'Summer.'"

"Well," she said. "Well, well."

They walked between rows of corn on a dirt road too narrow for the tow truck and the car. "If we stir up dust," he said, "we won't be able to see." The moon was out. They did not need lights. They walked quietly, at times in single file when the path narrowed, and other times shoulder to shoulder. Their hands brushed together twice, but barely, so insignificant it might have been imagined. There was a break in the corn.

"Follow me," he said.

They turned from the path and entered between the rows of crinkling papery husks, remnants of silk brushing their faces and necks, the stalks taller than either of them. Joanne pretended she was Jenny Almeter, lost but not lost. She was being guided by her own hands, white in the moonlight, held out away from her body and poised to part a row of corn or the entire field. Brian was leading the way, but still Joanne kept her hands raised, ready. Some kids had speculated that night: maybe Jenny went off into the corn with a boy. Someone who had snaked back, returned to the house without being seen. Or maybe she had been alone all along, pulled to a place the others were scared of. Joanne wondered why she herself had ever been afraid. She tried to recreate the feeling of some twenty years ago, but it was impossible. Tonight, out in the corn, everything felt so clear and new that she could not remember what she had felt yesterday. Or even this morning.

A slight incline led them to the crest of what was barely a hill. When Brian stopped, her hands bumped into his back. He turned his head briefly, and in his expression she saw the exhilaration she felt. A wordless complicity.

The corn opened suddenly into a clearing. It was the size of two basketball courts connected end to end. Their shoes hit stone, a plateau, smoothed flat by glaciers and forces larger than themselves. The rock glittered in the moonlight with the appearance of fine granite.

"Careful," he said, not for the first time that day. "Watch your shoes."

It wasn't granite but glass—dark glass, clear glass, milk glass, colored glass—all broken to bits and shining on the table of rock. The outside rim of the plateau was cleared, his designated walking space, and they stood there looking. The layers of glass piled to almost half a foot and the moon rays seemed to shine all the way to the bottom, so they saw all the colors mixed together and reflecting. Pieces of a milky-white lamp soaked up the moon. The broken round bottoms of drinking glasses and jelly jars looked like buttons on a bedspread.

"I've never seen anything like it," she said. "It's lovelier than Christmas. Lit up without any lights."

He crunched across the surface and emptied his bags of broken glass to the ground, attempting even distribution. He returned to her, motioning for her paper bag, which she gave him. He removed two wine bottles, green glass with the labels peeled off, and handed one to her. He stood so close she could smell his breath, like mint yet different, sharper, something she wanted to put a name to.

"Now smash it," he said.

Joanne was already raising the bottle over her head with both hands.

Paternity Test

After the show, Mutt wanted to talk. He always pointed out our band's errors, so I figured he would bring up that night's commotion as he was launching into his guitar solo, when two yahoos in the crowd threw beer bottles at the stage and the bouncer kicked them out. Distracted by the broken glass at my feet, I bungled a note or two on bass, nothing egregious. But this time, Mutt wanted to talk about Maggie. She was not my favorite subject. She had watched us play with her back to the wall, staring Mutt down. When he looked up at the end of the solo, Maggie was gone.

Mutt liked to have a beer after our shows, but I was drinking ice water, even more ready to leave now that he had cornered me. Same old song, Maggie's husband a bigwig, she was lonely, and he, Mutt, served as a couple nights' diversion when he was playing within a certain mile radius. She wouldn't drive too far for him. Her husband read the odometer, suspicious bastard. She usually waited for Mutt outside the show, or at the motel, but this time she only left a note under his windshield wiper, describing her situation and asking what she should do next. Maggie was not that young. Her husband was even older. Mutt was calm, philosophical, as he slipped the note into his jeans pocket. It wasn't her husband's, she wrote, because of the vasectomy. Maggie didn't know that it couldn't be Mutt's, either, because of the accident in his late twenties, nearly fifteen years ago. Medical malpractice. His lawyer was the best. Same firm as Maggie's husband. They were statewide.

So there was someone else besides Mutt being someone else. He guessed that she made a wrong guess. Mutt described the way her eyes used to light up when the band played "Your Love," covering The Outfield. Using your love, not losing it, was what the song was about. Effing catchy little song. Now, Mutt said, who was using who? Their arrangement was obviously not exclusive. Mutt didn't have another girlfriend, but technically he did have a wife. He was married on paper to Alison, who needed health insurance benefits, which Mutt fortunately had thanks to his day job driving a local truck route for a craft brewery. Alison lived with her girlfriend in a loft downtown. Jenny. Sometimes the three of them smoked pot together. Alison and Jenny's families had not met Mutt. They didn't know he existed. Well, Jenny's brother did, but he didn't know Mutt and Alison were married. Mutt knew Bobby—that's Jenny's brother's name, Bobby—because of the time Mutt pointed out to him who was selling grass at the club. Bobby called it grass. Mutt called it weed. Not my thing, but whatever gets you through the night. Once, Bobby pulled his car up to Mutt's window when he was parked outside Alison and Jenny's building and said, Hey, remember me? Thanks for hooking me up. Bobby delivered the grass to his sister's place. Once he left, Mutt went up and smoked with them. Alison had a painful degenerative disease of the joints, and medical marijuana was not covered on Mutt's/her insurance. Doctor, physical therapy, and massage were in-network, though. He had briefly dated Jenny ages ago, and they stayed friends, and when Alison needed insurance, well, hell. He was glad to marry her, if it helped.

Anyway, Mutt said. Maggie's note got him all effed up. Why was she picking him when the baby couldn't be his? And what did she want to do? She hadn't said.

"Why tell me this, Mutt?" I asked him, knowing where this might be headed but in no hurry to get there. Out the window, the frontage road ran parallel to the highway, cars zipping past in two directions across six lanes. I felt dizzy.

I had to get home by midnight or Deb would kill me. And, I had to take the twins to the orthodontist the next day. Pickup from school and no snack because of the braces. A car ride full of complaining. They would miss specials, and tomorrow was PE, their favorite, taught by a young guy named Bobby. I didn't ask Mutt if it was the same Bobby. I was tired after the gig, and Mutt insisted I have a drink when he ordered another. I stuck with ice water. He didn't push me. We had known each other since grade school. "Matthew" turned "Matt" turned "Mutt," because he had always been a sly dog with the girls in our class, even at age eleven, when he organized Truth or Dare with kissing at recess. Even in high school marching band, when Mutt Dawg—redundant—led the drumline and flirted with the entire flag corps. I played alto sax.

The twins weren't mine but I raised them like they were. Deb didn't mind the band, but she worked an early shift and hated when I woke her up. Midnight was our agreement. The kids slept like rocks; they were a nonissue. Deb wanted me to keep my word. Her ex had lacked any kind of follow-through whatsoever, so even though I'm pretty responsible, I have to be extra conscientious. I'm trying to curse less, again to counterbalance the ex, an otherwise OK dude. He upheld every other weekend custody, and really seemed to love Zeb and Josiah. He wasn't religious but grew up near Amish country and thought the names sounded powerful. His name was Tim. When we texted about him—me and Deb, that is—I always mistyped it as Tom, for some reason. It became our inside joke, but not in front of the boys.

Mutt was always Mutt, never Matt. Told me once while we were drinking that he was jealous of me, because he wanted and couldn't have a kid. The doctor said the chances were infinitesimal. Maybe you'll get them like I did, I said. He nodded, changed the subject. I was glad. We hadn't been close since he started up with Maggie, whose husband was Deb's brother. It was awkward. Their father, my father-in-law, was a big and scary dude, not affectionate, interrupted throughout family dinner, slamming his water glass down on the table to make a point. That kind of thing. He was also wildly protective of Deb, but lenient with Chip Jr., Maggie's husband. All three had piercing bright-blue eyes, though my mother-in-law's eyes were normal blue.

"You know who Maggie's seeing?" Mutt asked me. "Who else, I mean?"

I couldn't tell him that a few months back, Maggie's husband had asked for my help. Could I drive him to and from a doctor's appointment and let him rest on my couch for the day? I said sure. My brother-in-law didn't tell me what the appointment was for. But Chip Jr. told Deb, who told me. He had changed his mind and gotten the vasectomy reversed. He badly wanted children now; family legacy meant more to him than it had when he and Maggie first met. Of course he should've talked this through with Maggie. His wife. I almost told Maggie myself. Deb convinced me to stay out of it; this was between Maggie and Chip. Anyway, I was busy making the twins' Halloween costumes—they're going as robots, with cardboard boxes, duct tape, paint, knobs, the works. You have never seen two kids more geeked up about Halloween.

So here's what I did tell Mutt: I don't know if Maggie has someone on the side—besides you—but you want a kid, right? And an infinitesimal chance is still a chance. Maggie's gauging how invested you are. So after the baby's born, you could get a paternity test, if you care about knowing whether you're the biological father. There's ads on bus stop benches, it's like a hundred bucks. And if that part doesn't matter to you, you can be a dad no matter the biology. Tell Maggie you'll do this thing together. If she divorces Chip, she'll get money from the prenup. Not a lot, but some.

Mutt smiled, relieved. Of course I did not say: if the kid came out and looked like Chip Jr., things might be different for everybody involved.

Quarter to midnight and I was about to turn into a pumpkin. We walked out to the parking lot, and there was Maggie, leaning against Mutt's car.

"Mutt, you got that note?" she said in a low voice, ignoring me. Things had been weird between me and Maggie after too much wine at Christmas Eve two years ago, when she cornered me in the kitchen and suggested something I don't even want to repeat, which never happened but lurked between us all this time. That was the thing I feared Mutt was going to bring up. Thank God he hadn't.

"False alarm," Maggie told Mutt. "Tear it up." She glowed. Poor Mutt had tears in his eyes, I could tell, even in the dark.

Maggie did look at me then, like she was daring me to say something. I've never told anyone about the "Sexy Christmas" getup she offered to wear for me, with the intention that I would take it off. Oh God. She even texted some pictures. Which I eventually deleted, even though the images are burned on my brain. Yeah, I looked. I'm not a robot. Maybe I should've told Deb about this, but she and Maggie had their own issues. Maggie dated Deb's first boyfriend, their freshman year of high school—he had dumped Deb on a Tuesday, and was with Maggie by Friday night. Deb was still devastated by it, all these years later. Why make it worse between them? There was already enough tension at family dinners, especially for me. Every time the family got together, I wondered if anyone had overheard me and Maggie that night in the kitchen or believed that I was up to something shady. I wasn't.

There was something else. In the pictures, Maggie's pose was about what you would expect, same for the outfit. But her eyes, if you bothered to look? Haunted, wounded. Like she'd seen some shit, and she was upset with the one who showed her, who had to be the person taking the picture. That's what I tell myself. The pictures are long deleted, so I can't confirm one way or another. But I see the flicker of that look in her eyes sometimes. It haunts me.

In the parking lot, I said a fast goodbye to Mutt and Maggie and sped off, snuggling into bed beside Deb as the clock turned 12:01. It took me a while to fall asleep. Maggie was happy to be child-free, but Mutt? Poor guy. Maybe Alison and Jenny would have a baby. They could order sperm on the internet and he could be the uncle. Or maybe he would get lucky like me and meet a woman with kids. Like Zeb and Josiah, those goofs. In the backseat of my car were lengths of plastic accordion tubing, the kind you would connect to the end of a drainpipe. I planned to spray paint them silver. As I finally relaxed and my brain drifted to that spot of almost dreaming, I reminded myself to hide the tubing in the trunk before the kids saw it. I wanted to do a big reveal with the finished costume. The boys were going to flip over those robot arms. I couldn't wait to attach them.

Nothing and Nobody

Billy's ex-wife called to say she was on her way over to discuss a very important matter, which, if history was any indicator, could mean a decision between practically identical shades of red nail polish or a veterinary crisis for Buck, the pet dog Nancy treated like the child they'd never had.

His apartment's galley kitchen counters were stacked with pizza boxes and foil tins of semi-recent Chinese takeout; he gathered them all into a lawn and leaf bag. They had bought a hundred rolls to help Nancy's nephew's Boy Scout troop finance a trip to the Grand Canyon. Nancy got custody of Buck and their modest ranch house. Billy got the lawn and leaf bags. He didn't have a lawn, not anymore, but he did have about seventy more rolls to use before he would give in and buy regular kitchen-sized bags.

There was nothing in the cupboard to offer her, and three beers left in the fridge. Good, he thought: a glass of water it is. He held a spotted glass to the light, washed and rinsed it twice, and dried it with a clean towel.

Nancy knocked before trying the unlocked doorknob. A courtesy knock; Nancy thought all doors were open to her and took great offense when proven otherwise.

"Hello?" Her curly head poked around the doorframe. "Thank God you're home. I'm frantic right now."

He swigged from his newly-opened beer. "How's Buck-O the Wonder Dog?"

"A total pain in my ass," she said. "But fine. That beer looks tasty."

"My last one," he lied. "Water?"

She nodded, eyes narrowed. "Listen. Did you RSVP to the reunion yet? Are you bringing anyone?"

So that was the very important matter. He was relieved it wasn't anything to do with Buck, an aging Maltipoo, though he would rather talk about the dog than their fifteen-year class reunion. Most everybody from high school knew that they had divorced the year before. Nancy, no doubt, was here to put on the pressure: Act normal. Let's be friends. Lots of people split up amicably. Dammit, then just pretend.

Nancy was on the decorating committee, so the next hour would be a one-sided discussion about crepe vs. Mylar streamers, should the helium balloons have messages, were real flower centerpieces better than fake, what with allergy season and all.

"Are *you* taking anyone?" Billy asked. "How about old what's-his-name?" Billy knew Steve's name. Nancy had been dating him, a graduate of the rival high school, for two months.

"Steve refuses to wear a belt," Nancy stated. "The man needs a belt."

"I'm not planning on wearing one, either," Billy told her.

"Like I care if you wear one," she said.

Billy held up his palms, surrendering.

"I like him, OK?" Nancy said. "But he's super weird about our town. It's an old sports grudge. Wrestling. I mean, my *God*. We're in our *thirties*. Get over it." She studied her nails. "Anyway. You will never guess who did RSVP."

Billy scratched his head, mocking this trivia. "Sukie Jones."

"Of course Sukie. She does hot yoga now, so you know she'll be wearing some ridiculous leotard. But that's not who I mean."

"Darryl Edwards. Brandon Connolly. Terry St. Clair."

"Oh, fuck off." They were other classmates Nancy had dated in high school. "They're coming, too. Want the shock-of-the-century guest? Krumcake."

Billy covered his mouth with one hand, but couldn't quite hide the smile.

"Cecelia Krum?" he asked, voice squeaking.

God, he had always been clear as Saran Wrap. His insides quivering, like a bowl full of chicken salad left too long at the picnic. Cecelia Krum, she of the lithe limbs and Breck hair and slow-motion grace, beautiful Cecelia, which one could deduce by name alone, as there has never been an unbeautiful Cecelia. Even the few who are beauty-challenged grow into their lovely names with stoic fate.

Nancy was frowning at her nails. "Wonder if she's still a total freak show?"

Billy remembered her differently. Cecelia was not a freak. Far from it. All those years ago, Cecelia Krum had saved his life. And she didn't even know it.

On his way to the high school to look through old yearbooks, he wished he had not told Nancy that he would be in charge of the senior picture photo display. Though he lived three miles away, he hadn't been inside the building in years. The halls were the same beigy-green color, the lockers dented as ever. Mrs. McCannon presided over the reception desk as if she were part of the faux wood grain, as if she had never gotten up, not even for a bathroom break. It was summer, and she wore voluminous white culottes with a sleeveless turquoise blouse. She fanned her face with one hand when Billy crossed into her domain, and the flesh of her bare upper arms swung back and forth.

"AC's down for repair. You think they'd let us take a day off."

"Hi, Mrs. McCannon."

She squinted at him. "Remind me: what year were you?"

"Billy Northfield, class of '93," he said.

Her squint gave way to a boilerplate smile that showed she did not remember him. "Of course!" she said. "And what brings you back?"

He explained that he needed pictures for the reunion, framing the task in such a way that he managed to disparage Nancy, who had been their much-beloved senior class president. Nobody understood why Nancy Butler had wanted to marry Billy Northfield, not straight out of high school. Back then, Billy could barely believe his luck, either.

The secretary unlocked the yearbook office, escorting him to the filing cabinets. "I trust you," she said, winking on her way out. "Got to get back to my oscillating fan."

The files were grouped by year, then by club or activity, stopping in 2001. Digital photography took over, he guessed. His only camera was an old point-and-shoot that made pictures look like instantaneous artifacts, blurred edges compared to the crisp new digital imagery. He and Nancy had used the camera throughout their marriage, and looking at the photos now, it was as if someone had run their fingers through each print, smudging their lives.

He easily located a manila folder with all the senior portraits, relieved he wouldn't have to search manually for each of his two hundred and seventeen classmates, many of whom he was not eager to see in a few short days. He tucked the folder into his bag on the tiled floor and began opening the other drawers. Gymnastics, Key Club, the Spanish-Speaking Travel League. No sense in bothering to search for himself—he wasn't a joiner. His was a club of one, a club of video games in his parents' unfinished basement.

This office housed forgotten memories, or ones he hadn't had access to. He knew Cecelia Krum lived inside at least some of those files, waiting like a paper doll. Waiting for him to find her, is how he thought of it. It was, admittedly, a stretch. Cecelia didn't know how much she meant to him, had never known, and if the gods of courage and foolhardiness were paying attention to him on Saturday, he would finally tell her about how she had changed his mind, how her mere presence in his life had convinced him of his worth. You had to tell people they mattered. You had to be specific. He knew that now.

It was senior year. Billy had gotten into the habit of skipping sixth period. The previous semester had been the big academic crunch, the one that guidance counselors threatened would make or break the rest of your life. Break your shot at college, at least, which Billy had no intention of attending. Still. At the beginning of the year he had shyly brought up a couple schools he was interested in to Mr. Loggia, his assigned counselor. This was a cross between bravery and bravado. His parents had never pushed him to be any more than what they were: high school graduates spending their lives behind brooms. Mr. Loggia had told Billy with little preamble or gentleness that each college pick would be a stretch for someone like him. Billy had taken an awful lot of the vocational classes, Mr. Loggia tried helpfully. Plenty of good mechanics in town. And though Billy had wound up at Pitzler Brothers Brakes & Muffler, and was relatively happy, he refused to offer his counselor any of the credit. What right did that man have to dissuade him from college? He was unlikely to have gone, anyway, but that wasn't the point.

Someone like him. What did that phrase even mean, Billy had scorned inside, a thought mixed with deep hurt and emotion. Because he knew what it meant. In 1992, he was the type they would call a loner, isolated. He owned an awful lot of black clothing, years before such a guise was ominous, soon-to-be-infamous. He was just a quiet teenager who couldn't articulate his loneliness, so he wore it instead: black T-shirts, dark jeans, black high-tops.

The school had yet to keep its doors locked during the day, had never discussed emergency plans to deal with a mass tragedy or a school shooter. Billy wasn't scary, just a kid who had "slipped through the cracks." In 1992, that described a variety of students: geeks, potential high achievers who strayed, jocks who forfeited scholarship opportunities because of alcohol and pot. The phrase was a consolation for teachers and principals: We can't reach everybody. Parents must take accountability. Blah, blah, blah. In Billy's junior year, Nancy Butler, with whom he shared Painting II, had toyed with his emotions for a marking period before choosing someone else. Friendless and girlfriendless and without a plan for the future, Billy knew he wasn't slipping anywhere. He *was* the cracks.

Sixth-period chemistry was no great loss. It was the kind of class that led you to other classes, which led you to college, where Billy wasn't headed. Not someone like him. He had begun spending the period on the flat school roof, a tar papered surface that almost hissed in the sun. A ladder snaked up through the drama department's musty props closet, empty this time of day. He could've gone out to the woods beyond the baseball diamond, or walked the few short blocks to the strip mall, where he could get a pizza slice. Funny, though, that he stayed close to school. That he wanted to be up high, gaining another viewpoint, even if it remained his own. Here on the roof he collected his thoughts and planned for the short-term future.

He did not want to go to the trouble of a gun. The fingerprinting, the permit, the money he did not have. He worried about procuring pills and whether pills would work. Any type of bloodletting meant a horror-show mess someone would have to clean up, and he had always been considerate, as well as squeamish about razors.

In the drama department, there was a rope.

A lasso made from someone's parents' old sailing supplies, likely leftover from an ancient production of *Oklahoma!* The school hung onto each prop and gown for the inevitable return of each musical, staged in a different year with different kids with pretty much the same result. For a week straight, Billy had taken the lasso from its hook, careful to rearrange the feather boas and rubber exercise bands (for what production were those used?), and each day he would descend from the roof and replace the rope. Sometimes he put it back in a slightly different place: in front of the boas instead of behind them, say. He imagined he was the only one who noticed.

One overcast Friday when he ascended the ladder, the trapdoor to the roof was wide open. He debated climbing the last several rungs, afraid he might disturb someone, perhaps a janitor or maintenance worker who would report him to the principal. Then he wondered if he had accidentally left the door open the day before. It was possible: though he had envisioned the end result (the thick metal pipe as an anchor, the length needed to go over the edge), his actions were more like bread crumbs than actual plotting. Deep in his heart, he was asking, *Find me.*

Instead Billy found Cecelia Krum, smoking a cigarette on the eastern edge of the roof. He approached slowly and dumbly, the lasso coiled around his arm, and saw she merely held an unlit cigarette between her fingers. She was staring over the edge of the one-story building. Her right leg dangled over the side. His shoe caught a pebble, which skittered away, and Cecelia looked up sharply with violet eyes, both dark and bright simultaneously against the gray sky. The far horizon was deep gray-green; "tornado sky," his mother called it. A sharp delineation between the clouds and the nothing below them.

They said nothing for a moment, which is rarer than you might think. Especially for high schoolers, who subsist on the speed of their edgy, attention-seeking speech. Cecelia broke the silence after a long minute, tapping what Billy saw was a pen, not a cigarette, on a folded newspaper.

"What's a four-letter word for sand-dwelling creature?" she asked.

Normally Billy would've stammered an apology and backed away, feeling like an intruder. But he was possessive of the roof. All week, it had been his and his alone. And while he wanted to be alone, he also had to acknowledge how much he wanted to enjoy the vision of Cecelia sitting on the roof's edge, her long leg swinging, her shiny chestnut hair tangling in the ticklish wind, her violet eyes. They had been in school together for years but scarcely had talked. He knew she had a gaggle of younger siblings, offered up as an excuse for why she couldn't complete the essay on Hester Prynne or why she dropped out of activities after a single meeting or practice. Mr. Loggia's impassioned speech to Cecelia Krum was guidance counselor legend. Her test scores were off the charts, so how can you fail Algebra 2, Loggia asked, with logic results like hers? There's no reason for it.

"There is if you don't go to class," Cecelia had said, executing said skills.

The tar paper roof was merely warm instead of piping hot. A trickle of sweat inched down Billy's back. He wanted to ask if she skipped class often, but in his head it sounded corny, like a pickup line. Instead, he answered her crossword question.

"How about 'crab'?" he asked.

She appraised him. "Not too shabby."

Billy remained immobile.

"You can come closer. I do bite, but I won't."

Instant boner. He moved the rope from his arm, positioning it strategically in front of him. He walked closer, and gingerly sat upon the two-foot high wall at the roof's edge. Cecelia's leg still swung, and dangling from her foot was a navy blue and white polka-dotted espadrille. He worried her shoe would fall off. It would land on the sidewalk near the gymnasium entrance.

"What's that for?" she asked, then shook her head as if she didn't want to know. Billy suddenly couldn't remember why he had a rope, either, or where it had come from. Somewhere inside, he might've realized that a suicide claims more than one life, even if no one else dies.

"Found it," he said.

"I wasn't going to jump," she announced. "I couldn't deal with English today. You have Mrs. Sheedy? No? You're lucky. She's got it out for me."

Billy listened intently. He did not want to say the wrong thing. He did not want to send this creature scampering back down the ladder. He needn't have worried. Cecelia did the talking for both of them.

"A crossword's better than class, if you asked me," she said. "Works your brain differently. Makes you more clever, you know? Mrs. Sheedy is clever in a kind of gross way. Like, so smart that her humor goes over most everybody's head, and those of us who get it become her mangy little pets. Some days she'll zone in on me for the entire fifty minutes. Have you ever been stared at for so long you feel like your head's about to burst into flames? *Foosh!*"

She gestured with both hands to show her head exploding. Billy laughed and looked at the ground; he probably was staring at Cecelia in much the same way. The talk felt natural, and they knew each other from a lifetime of attending the same small town schools. But this was the first real conversation they had ever had, one on one. Back in third grade, Billy had joined a group of boys in chasing Cecelia Krum around the playground, shouting variations of her name. What a fool he had been.

"Maybe you don't remember, but I was one of the kids who called you Krumcake," he said. "But I meant it kind of nicely. Cake's one of my favorite foods."

She laughed, and her perfect, small white teeth flashed. "Forget it," she said. "We were all tiny little babies. Hey, where are you supposed to be now, anyway?"

Billy smiled for what felt like the first time in ages. "Here," he said.

The yearbook office's clock ticked as loudly as a bomb, just as it had fifteen years ago when the students waited for it to go off. Some things, most things, did not change.

Like Billy's mental image of Cecelia Krum. He licked the sweat from his upper lip. He had dug up a half-dozen photos of her. Mostly candids, and who looks their best in candids? Still. He had remembered her grace, balancing on the school's roof, the way she lightly dangled her leg. The photo of her playing badminton in a gym class action shot, however, revealed a figure best described as gawky. Her limbs were a geometry problem, her racket a weapon. Her T-shirt, red with a white strip for markering one's name, said KRUM in blocky letters. In another unflattering portrait, she could be seen in the crowded cafeteria line, gazing with disdain at a smiling couple in an embrace. Tonya Whitson and Brad Chamberlain, who, admittedly, were a sickeningly sweet pair. Had she been against public display of affection? Did she hold a grudge against Tonya, or a crush on Brad? Vice versa? In her scowl he recognized the feelings he had held at that age, uncomfortably so. He saw her face contorted and her nose a bit smushed and her teeth more crooked than he had remembered. Unsettling, to say the least, that his memory was so far from these snapshots.

They were just pictures, he reminded himself, thumbing through the senior yearbook, wanting the reassurance of her color portrait, her violet eyes. You got to select from proofs which shot made the yearbook, though that made little difference for him—his photo never quite came out right. Most kids dressed up; he had worn a concert T-shirt in support of a band he now was embarrassed to have liked. He bypassed his own photo and stared at Cecelia. She stared back, frank and challenging, and he thought he detected a hint of disdain. He logically knew it was for the photographer, not him, but at the moment it felt more like a reproach coming from those eyes. Cecelia's irises were brown.

They had finished the crossword and turned their faces skyward, absorbing the weak sunlight that made a brief appearance. Cecelia blinked rapidly in the sun, giving Billy the notion that she was batting her eyes at him. (He amended the memory: batting her brown eyes.) Her next period was band, where she was learning classical guitar. She wouldn't miss it. Was he coming?

He sighed. Of course the afternoon couldn't last forever. Why was it the class period dragged interminably when you were seated at a desk, but passed in a blur if you happened to be skipping class with a beautiful girl on top of the roof? (His current mind replaced Cecelia the vision with

Cecelia the scowler, and he shook his head, as she had done, to clear the thought as if from an Etch-a-Sketch toy.)

"Suppose I ought to go to class," he said. "Even if it's study hall."

"Let me go first," she said, her hand on the ladder, and Billy, his boner now becalmed, took the chance to gather the rope and sling it over his arm.

When they both stood on the firm ground of the prop closet, Cecelia reached forward and gave his shoulder a little squeeze. Really, she was taking the lasso gently away from him. Her movement caused the feather boas to ruffle soundlessly, placidly, like sea anemones underwater.

"The rope goes behind the boas," she said. "Not in front." Her voice was absent of contempt or scolding. Her words carried no judgment. But she had noticed his small gesture, and his sense of humanity turned on its ear. She had noticed *him*.

Several weeks passed, and he had curried favor with Nancy again, lifting his funk even as his mother warned him against "that Butler girl." He had stopped going up to the roof, and had stopped thinking about the rope and how it could be used. He marveled at the easy absence of those thoughts. Eventually, walking by the drama department triggered his memory: he finally saw other meaning in Cecelia's words. She, too, had known the exact location of that prop. I wasn't going to jump, she had said. At the time, he viewed her comment through his own depressed vision. Later, he understood her differently, and saw how he had failed: the words were hers to be reflected back, not absorbed by him as smugly as a suntan.

"Too many pictures of the Krumcake," Nancy said Saturday morning, her fingers dunked in sudsy water. She had summoned Billy to the manicurist to check his progress on the photo project. Her splayed hands twitched as Lisa Macomber, two years ahead of them in school, filed and trimmed. Lisa studiously ignored their conversation, which is to say absorbed every word silently and tucked it away in her internal hard drive. She would later retrieve dates, details and names for any client who summoned an associative phrase.

"Huh," Billy said. "I've got plenty of everybody."

"What a nobody, that girl. Kind of a hippie. Wasn't she all into the environment?"

"Everybody cares about the environment."

"They do now. But back then? What a weird thing for a teenager to obsess over: pop bottles and Styrofoam McNuggets boxes."

Billy thought it simply offered more proof of Cecelia's empathetic nature. He tried not to think of her giving the stink eye to the couple in the cafeteria line.

Nancy wouldn't give the photo display a rest. "And you can put this together by tonight? Billy, I'm counting on you. We're doing the cocktail hour first, and the early birds will be drinking mixers in the parking lot before we're even ready. I need to have stuff set up, like, yesterday."

"I'll bring it when I come," he said. "You know, make a grand entrance."

She narrowed her eyes, taking in his new haircut. "You aren't bringing a date, are you?"

"No."

"Then who're you trying to impress?"

"You, Nancy," he said, staring directly at Lisa Macomber, whose mouth hung open. He had installed the manicurist's new brakes last month, and she talked on her cell phone the whole time, even as he processed her credit card. "It's always you, my darling ex-wife."

"Oh, shut up," Nancy said. "And be there by six."

From the start of their married life, Billy and Nancy had fought over everything. Money and in-laws, sure, those were a given. But they bickered over the name of an actor in a commercial. What to order on their pizza. Which movie to rent from Blockbuster. They had never discussed having kids, and when it finally came up, they fought about that, too. Billy wanted children. Nancy did not. Kids would change everything, she said. Not long after that, Nancy came home at 3:00 a.m., sobbing over Brandon Connolly rejecting her. Billy thought she had meant back in high school. It was a few weeks before he found out she had meant that night, at the bar, and now it was over between them.

Billy's nerves wore him raw all afternoon, thinking of seeing Cecelia, wondering what she would be like. Would she match the pictures in his head, or the pictures he had taken from the yearbook office? Fifteen years after graduation, she was probably someone else entirely now. But who? And how had *he* changed? Nancy, enmeshed in the last-minute preparations of the reunion, was his most reliable source for this last question, and unavailable for comment. His worry nagged at him until finally he sank into a deep, dreamless sleep on the blue velvet couch. When he woke, it was six thirty. He still hadn't assembled the photo display, hadn't even opened Nancy's shrink-wrapped poster board from Schafer's Art Supply.

Nobody needs a photo display, he decided, quickly dressing in his one and only suit, black, with a deep-blue satin tie. He could sort of scatter the photos on one of the linen-draped lunch tables. He would deal with Nancy later.

His new haircut was not bad. He scrubbed his hands extra hard and stuck his nails into the bar of Ivory, digging around for maximum cleanliness. He was a man who still performed menial tasks for his unfaithful ex-wife. He was a reliable mechanic and a sound sleeper. He liked his burgers well-done and could not stand whiskey, a taste he no longer tried to acquire. He had learned, over the years, to please himself. He was learning.

He was not a high school senior standing on a roof. He was not a high school senior standing on a roof. He was not. Or if he was, if that part of him remained, then that wasn't all he was.

Cecelia Krum packed light for the reunion; she only planned to stay one night. Kath lay on their bed, supervising wardrobe choices.

"Who were the hot girls in your class?" Kath teased. "Come on. You know you had a secret crush."

Cecelia held up a blue dress to her body and frowned. "I really didn't," she said. "Is that weird?"

"Not weird, just surprising," Kath said. "I was in love with all the female teachers. Half the senior class. All of the cheerleaders. The softball team."

Cecelia smiled at her in the mirror. "Such a cliché."

Kath held up her middle finger, touched it to her lips, and blew Cecelia a kiss. "Wear your silver dress. Especially if you want to be remembered as a smokin' hot fox."

Cecelia did wonder how people remembered her, one reason she was going back. She recalled high school as one long standardized test. A test without directions, without the required Number 2 pencils, without measurable outcomes. The standards—not the state mandates passed down from on high, but the everyday ones by which students were expected to live—baffled her. She thought she was providing the right answer until a teacher would ridicule her. She liked her new haircut until another student whispered about it being so *choppy*, and she refused to have it cut for the remainder of the year, which caused her peers to label her a hippie. They followed at a close distance in the hallway, watching her every move, and she, in turn, watched them, wondering what on earth she could possibly be doing wrong. "See how she walks," one girl whispered to another, and magically, Cecelia had new material to add to her list: Reasons for Being Self-Conscious, a list she actually kept in her red, spiral-bound notebook, which she refused to call a diary or a journal. That's what it was, though: the material with which she built the case of her life. Ways she learned to build cases for and against other lives.

As she jotted her musings on the various characters in her school—that's how she thought of them, as characters—certain patterns emerged. Being in the gaze of others caused her great upset. At some point, maybe junior year, she had exhausted herself with the possibilities of what her class- mates could possibly think, or want, from her. She wouldn't describe it as numbness, exactly; more like massive detachment. Unconsciously she adopted a new attitude: what was wrong with being observed? And: if people were watching, then put on a show.

Her voice grew louder and echoed through the halls. She started wear- ing colored contact lenses, and stared down anyone who glanced twice. Sometimes she would bark, just for fun. Her long hair no longer was repa- ration for a botched haircut but a choice. An extension of herself, some- times piled on top of her head, sometimes hanging limply, unbrushed. She did not, would not, care. She was treated differently. Noticed. This time, praised. Some girls mimicked her; others critiqued those who adopted fickle, Cecelia-inspired fashions. But they stopped criticizing Cecelia.

She took notes in her red notebook, a practice in sociological field study that would prove useful in her government job. How much, she wondered, would be too much to reveal? She was rehearsing conversations for the reunion. There had been humanitarian work, which sometimes involved acts of mercy. Mercenary? That wasn't quite right, either. She planned to stay only one night in her old hometown, then she would drive her rental car back to O'Hare for an early Sunday flight back to DC. Back to her life with Kath, and the Georgetown townhome they had shared for the last two years.

Cecelia's family had moved shortly after graduation, and she hadn't returned to her old town. She had been married once, just out of college. A mistake. She and Pedro split up two weeks before their year anniversary. Meeting Kath, she told their friends, was like coming home to a dream house she never knew she wanted to live in.

"You might want to take these." Kath unfurled a strand of foil-wrapped condoms.

"Please tell me those are vintage," Cecelia said.

Kath signed the letters "AL," which was their code for "Another Life." The lives they lived before meeting each other.

Kath was an American Sign Language interpreter for the deaf. She worked events at the White House and the Kennedy Center; you could see her on television, her lovely, expressive hands moving as if to mimic flight. Cecelia, who had not come out to her parents and siblings, let alone her high school class, was relieved Kath had to work that weekend. She would be signing at a Paul Simon concert. Her favorite song was "50 Ways to Leave Your Lover." Kath and Cecelia would listen to it in bed and murmur, *Another Life.*

Sign language interpreter was a great job to bring up at a high school reunion. Cecelia didn't know how to talk about her own work. She had traveled the world on the government's dime, translating, healing, performing jobs that involved keeping silent. Cecelia was paid to be silent. Kath finally had stopped asking.

She could not talk about Miles, an agent she had known since her first assignment in Haiti, though they only spoke or emailed sporadically in the last few years. He had returned from Iraq, the picture of cheer for exactly one week. Smiling and drinking and barhopping, sleeping it off. On the eighth day, he hung himself in the basement with an orange electrical cord. His wife found the body. She would not permit anyone from the government to attend the funeral. Cecelia understood that she could not have saved Miles. But she would've attended the services, would've paid a thousand dollars for the last-minute flight to Milwaukee.

When the class reunion e-vite arrived a few months later, she had impulse-booked a bargain flight home. She could not talk about her work. No. There were safe topics: the skeletal infant with AIDS transformed into a chubby-cheeked toddler who loved sticky rice. The teenager who had lost his right leg to a land mine, who now lectured at American high schools, and had appeared on the *Today* show. Her life, she realized, was probably more interesting than most of her classmates' lives. Probably. What did she know? She was just the Krumcake, or Environment Girl, or BHD for Bad Hair Day. At least before. Pre-detachment. Some of the boys in her class had gone straight to the military and had been deployed all over the world. In some ways, Cecelia thought she had done the same thing, well before that flight to Haiti after her last college exam. Even back in high school: she deployed herself elsewhere. It was a mental trick, daydreaming in class and doodling in a notebook. Other times, she needed the perspective from the roof.

Cecelia had been going to the roof alone for ages before Billy Northfield showed up. He never saw her. There was a brick chimney to crouch behind, and she would use a compact mirror to check him out. She wasn't all that hidden, and sometimes she worried he caught the sun's glare from her mirror, but mostly he seemed absorbed in his thoughts and the old lasso from *Oklahoma!* (she had been an extra), threading it through his palms as if he were a deckhand. Billy Northfield, whose ears had stuck out until ninth grade when he finally grew into them, and his huge nose, a real honker, which no one mentioned because Billy wasn't the type that people at their school noticed. If you were quiet, if you were thoughtful, if you were the slightest bit off-kilter—and this is how Cecelia perceived Billy, and to a lesser degree, herself—you were either traumatized or completely unseen. Either way, you were made to feel like nothing, a nobody. They were not friends. They never spoke until that day on the roof.

Cecelia set the whole thing up. She knew his routine and had grown nervous that he was considering expanding upon it. The next step. The final solution. His eyes grew flat as buttons. She had seen him at lunch, untouched cheeseburger on his cafeteria tray, so absorbed with that dingbat Nancy Butler. In English, Nancy had claimed *The Great Gatsby* was a magician, and in history, declared that the atom bomb was named after its creator, "Adam Somebody."

Cecelia actually brushed her hair that day. She wore her contacts. She perched comfortably on the ledge and lured him over and talked him down, as it were. She felt euphoric. Addicted. The look he had given her, the pureness of his gratitude, the innocence she knew he possessed, and by turn, that she possessed. He had recognized something in her that she didn't know existed. It was like being a child again. She had never told anyone or tried to explain what had happened that day; how could they comprehend it? She barely understood. He was the first to change her like that. *My first,* she sometimes thought of him in her head.

Billy had gone back to mooning over Nancy; she heard they had gotten married. After the roof, they never really spoke again, though once or twice they exchanged nods in the school hallways. It wasn't romantic, which she supposed didn't matter. Cecelia had paid him scant attention before the rooftop encounter, and it would be years before she understood that her lack of interest in men might mean she was actually interested in women. But she noticed the way he looked at her. She saw him try to hide his erection, a move nearly any high school girl could decipher. After that, he was on her mind constantly. She daydreamed about the ways he might show his gratitude, simultaneously chastising her own sappiness. She longed for a mixtape, a midnight hike through silent suburbs, a drive along country roads with nothing but corn surrounding them. She retreated in her mind from the chaos of her seven younger brothers and sisters, understanding that her mild fantasies had little to do with Billy. She didn't know what music he liked. She didn't know if he had a car. It was this: thinking about him allowed her to think about herself.

Even so. The way she saw herself was through his eyes. His was the face she saw nightly in her mind's eye. Even now, she saw his expression of wonder and relief, and yes, say it: love. A look caused by her, given to her. Her first.

"What are you thinking about?" Kath asked. "Or should I say, who are you thinking about?"

Miles, Billy, herself: whatever her answer, Kath wouldn't quite understand. It was better to gloss over certain things.

"Nothing and nobody," Cecelia said. "No lost loves, no love lost. Promise." Cecelia hugged Kath goodbye, and hoisted the roller suitcase down the stairs. It was heavy, but she was stronger than she looked.

At the reunion, the Class of 1993 had had enough of "Baby Got Back" by the third playing. The first time around, the crowd grew raucous and shook it like there was no tomorrow. The second time, the dancing turned ironic. Now the DJ was a few drinks in, and Nancy marched over and practically yanked the young man's ear. She grabbed the microphone while the DJ scrambled for a new song.

"Please be sure to stop by the picture *table*," she told the crowd. "Sorry there isn't a more attractive display."

Their senior prom song came on: "Wonderful Tonight" by Eric Clapton. It had been held in this very gym, and for the reunion Nancy recreated the same color scheme of peach and gold. The after-prom party at Sukie's was where Billy and Nancy had sex for the first time. Now Nancy stared at Billy with soft eyes—was she drunk? Tearful, even?—and Billy touched the stash of photos in his suit coat's interior breast pocket.

As if summoned, Cecilia was before him.

"Billy?" she asked, and he relished being both the question and the answer.

She was lovelier than he had dared dream, in a silver dress and black patterned tights and heels that gave her several inches on him. She hugged him, and he breathed in her gardenia perfume. What did he smell like to her? He hoped not the beer he had gulped earlier, waiting out the first playing of Sir Mix-A-Lot.

"I'm superglad to see you," she said. "Dance with me?"

How to explain that this was his and Nancy's song? From prom fifteen years ago? He felt sorry for his ex-wife, who eyed them from her perch at the punch bowl. Sukie, indeed in a leotard-like dress, edged closer to Billy and Cecelia, pretending not to listen.

His heart said Yes! Of course! His mouth said, "I shouldn't."

Cecelia's face fell. She didn't know why she had asked him to dance. Kath would say she was taking herself too seriously. She had a strong urge to call her, to hear Kath chuckle at Cecelia's familiar lack of social graces. Kath could remind her that Miles and Billy were not the same person, if she had known either of them existed.

"Right," she said. She glanced toward the door and squeezed her clutch. "Could you excuse me a second?"

She was out the door. Nancy saw an opening and sauntered over. "You aren't going to ask me to dance? Not even for old times' sake?"

Billy stared after Cecelia. "No," he said. "There are lots of other old timers who'll dance with you."

Nancy no longer appeared sentimental; she reverted to her default setting of pissed off. Sukie burst out laughing. "Damn, Billy."

His instinct was to apologize. Instead, he walked away.

Of course Cecelia was on the roof. She was flicking her lighter like an early '80s concertgoer. He cleared his throat so as not to startle her.

"Play 'Free Bird,'" she commanded.

He smiled. "Nah, I don't know it. Look, I'm really sorry. Do you remember Nancy?"

She snorted. "Was Adolf Hitler a Japanese kamikaze pilot?"

He ignored the jab. "We got divorced last year. That was our prom song."

She turned deadpan. "Shit. I ruined prom. Just like in *Carrie*."

"The pigs' blood was overkill," he said.

"Tell it to Stephen King." She flicked the lighter again. "Sorry. I'm divorced, too. We didn't even last a year."

"What happened?"

She shrugged. "My girlfriend says I was repressed."

He nodded like he knew. "Wait, what?"

Should she have said lover, partner, something else? She had little practice using these words. Her far-flung family still didn't know that she and Kath were more than roommates, more than friends. "Tell them we're lez-be-friends," Kath suggested.

"My girlfriend," Cecelia told Billy. "We live together in DC. Kath's amazing."

"That's cool," he said, too quickly.

Billy and Cecelia turned shy then, remembering other overly intimate conversations. They knew each other best in their imaginations.

"Hey," he said. "I have something for you." He produced the photograph of her in the cafeteria line, scowling at Tonya and Brad's public display of affection. Of course she would make that face, Billy thought, now that he knew she had been in the closet. He had assumed that his and Cecelia's desire to disappear was of the same variety.

"God, is that even me?" She smiled, with an unreadable expression beneath the surface. This much-anticipated moment was no match for memory, for their shared, deep longing for the survived past. They wouldn't dance together tonight, or any night. They wouldn't exchange confidences or email addresses, or stumble out in the dark night air of the parking lot, where the aged jocks were smoking cigars. They would return to their lives. They would adjust the antennas on their static-filled memories.

Cecelia held up the lighter and squinted at this version of herself from fifteen years ago. She pointed to a figure cropped half out of the frame, someone Billy failed to notice. One big ear, half a large nose. It was him, staring off camera at something impossible to discern, then or now. And here he was, standing before her, alive on the very roof where he had contemplated death.

Cecelia cried out, tears in her eyes, and then she was laughing. Billy joined in. They laughed and laughed, almost uncontrollably. They leaned on the wall to hold themselves up.

"Do you remember when that was taken?" he asked. His planned admission—*You saved me*—stalled in his throat. The momentous words he had rehearsed now seemed over-the-top, too large for the roof and the open sky above them.

Cecelia propped her elbows on the ledge and lit the lighter again. "Circa the Bad Hair era. Yo, Northfield. Bring that terrible little time capsule closer."

He dangled it over the roof's edge to the waiting flame. She looked at him. "Ready?"

"No," he said. "I want to say thanks first. So, thanks." His face went scarlet, hoping she understood. In a way, she did.

She laughed, heart as full as it had ever been. "You're very welcome. Thank *you*."

He nodded: *Go*. Paper met flame. The photograph curled in bright shades of orange and blue, the ash disappearing into the dark night air. Bits of nothing into nothing. It was impossible to see the tiny flecks' path. Back in high school, he would've assumed that the ashes fell, not taking into account height and wind, the angle of the flame, the person lighting the fire. Now Billy understood what Cecelia had known all along, even if she needed reminding. First they rose.

Acknowledgments

Thank you to Dennis Lloyd, Jackie Krass, and the entire team at University of Wisconsin Press. What a pleasure to return to Wisconsin, state of my birth, via this story collection.

Many thanks to the editors who published several of these stories in literary magazines, especially Jennifer Pashley, who selected "Hysterectomy" for *Stone Canoe*'s Allen and Nirelle Galson Prize for Fiction.

The IUPUI English Department has been a supportive home for my writing and teaching. With this book, I owe particular thanks to Rob Rebein, Megan Musgrave, Carrie Sickmann, Karen Kovacik, Missy Kubitschek, Terry Kirts, Hannah Haas, Mitchell L. H. Douglas, Kyle Minor, Steve Fox, and David Hoegberg.

I am also grateful to the friends and teachers who helped me imagine and reimagine these stories over the course of many years: Barney Haney, Porter Shreve, Sharon Solwitz, Patricia Henley, Bryan Furuness, Barbara Shoup, Susan Neville, Melissa Fraterrigo, Janine Harrison, and Michael Poore. I appreciate the feedback and moral support, not to mention the occasional snack.

Special thanks to Charlotte Shoulders, Julie Heger, Danielle Bethke, and Jennifer Murphy for cheering me and these stories on. I am holding close the memory of dear friends Paige Muellerleile, Carrie Urton McCaw, and Susan Jackson Learned, all greatly missed and remembered with love.

Thank you to my family for all your encouragement: Terri Layden, Katie Robbins, Audrey and Olivia Robbins, Eileen and Sam LaMarca, and Patricia Murphy.

There's no one I'd rather be locked down with during a pandemic than my husband, Tom Murphy, and our wonderful children, Trevor and Brendan. Lucky me.

John Layden, my late father, was an electrical engineer at Schlitz for thirteen years and earned an MBA at UW–Milwaukee. He would have gotten such a kick out of the University of Wisconsin Press publishing this book. Sometimes the universe winks big.